I0630709

MARRYING BONNIE

Brides of Clearwater: Book Four

MELANIE D. SNITKER

DALLIONE MEDIA, LLC

Marrying Bonnie
(Brides of Clearwater: Book Four)
By Melanie D. Snitker

All rights reserved
© 2020 Melanie D. Snitker

Dallionz Media, LLC
P.O. Box 643
Boerne, TX 78006

Cover Image: Jennifer Pitts Photography
https://www.jenniferpittsphotography.com/

Cover: Blue Valley Author Services
http://www.bluevalleyauthorservices.com/

Edited By: Krista Burdine at Grammaresque
https://iamgrammaresque.com/

All rights reserved. No part of this publication may be reproduced, distributed, or transmitted in any form or by any means, including photocopying, recording, or other electronic or mechanical methods, without the prior written permission of the author, except in the case of brief quotations embodied in critical reviews and certain other noncommercial uses permitted by copyright law.

Please only purchase authorized editions.

For permission requests, please contact the author at the email below or through her website.

Melanie D. Snitker
melanie@melaniedsnitker.com
www.melaniedsnitker.com

This is a work of fiction. Names, characters, businesses, places, events, and incidents either are the products of the author's imagination or used in a fictitious manner. Any resemblance to actual persons, living or dead, or actual events is purely coincidental.

Chapter One

onnie Tabor eased her red Volkswagen Passat into a parking space and turned off the engine. As soon as she opened the rear passenger door, her young charge, Gunner, kicked his feet in anticipation, as though the motion might somehow free him sooner. Bonnie smiled at his enthusiasm. "Hold on, buddy." She released the car seat harness and lifted the two-and-a-half-year-old boy into her arms. He immediately began to squirm as he tried to get down.

"You can walk when we get across the parking lot." She pressed a kiss to Gunner's cheek and shifted him in her arms. Once she retrieved a small backpack, she closed and locked the car again.

Gunner may not be her son, but she'd been his nanny since he was three months old. Spending nearly every weekday with the little guy had resulted in a strong bond between them. She could honestly say she loved her job and the child she cared for.

Even if his single father, Jace Echolls, often drove her crazy with his unpredictable work schedule. She'd go insane if she didn't regularly have Saturdays and Sundays off. Oh, and a more than decent paycheck. She belonged to a nanny group online, and while she didn't share her own salary, she was made aware of how thankful she should be for what Jace paid her.

Still, when he pulled stunts like the one tonight, it aggravated her to no end. Jace was a workaholic, and his occasional disregard for her personal time was annoying.

It was Friday evening, and Bonnie should be at her apartment getting ready for a date. Instead, Jace had informed her of a last-minute meeting that would delay him from returning home for at least two more hours. He could have at least asked her if she had plans first instead of assuming.

Which meant Bonnie's workday had been extended.

Normally, she wouldn't have minded as much. Having extra money in the bank account was always good. But tonight, she was supposed to meet her boyfriend, Lew, for dinner. She first suggested they go out Saturday night instead, but he'd insisted it had to be Friday. To say Lew was less than happy about the change in plans was an understatement.

She flinched at the memory of his sharp words over the phone.

"It's one thing to be dedicated to your job, Bonnie. But this is different. You let your boss have complete control of your time. I'm starting to wonder if it's only the kid you really care about."

Bonnie had hesitated, completely shocked at his words. "What do you mean?"

Apparently, he'd taken the delay as possible confirmation and snorted. "Nothing, Bonnie. I'll talk to you next week. Assuming you can work me into your schedule."

With that, the connection ended, and Bonnie had woodenly pocketed her phone.

His assessment of her hadn't been fair. It's not like any of this was a surprise since he knew she worked as a nanny from the day they met. She was completely free every weekend, and she spoke to Lew on the phone most evenings. Her schedule was more reliable than his. She never knew which evenings he was free until he called and asked her out. He should've been speaking into a mirror with his accusations of being too dedicated to one's job.

Even worse, it was ridiculous that Lew would insinuate she had feelings for Jace. Jace kept his personal life and business—the category Bonnie fell into—completely separate. Bonnie was his employee, and while Jace had always been kind, he'd made it clear multiple times that was exactly the way he wanted it.

Sure, maybe she had developed a serious crush on the guy six months after she started working for him, but she'd pushed that away. The last thing she needed was to jeopardize what she considered the perfect job because she acted like a teenager. She was thirty-one years old with a great job and a boyfriend—even if he had been a first-class jerk earlier.

Besides, poor Jace lost his wife to a pulmonary embolism just days after Gunner was born. All Bonnie knew about the woman was that her name was Samantha, and from the one picture of her in Gunner's room, she was truly beautiful.

Jace never spoke about her. For all Bonnie knew, he was still hopelessly in love with his wife and grieved daily for her. If that were the case, he was definitely off-limits.

Shoving thoughts of Jace aside, and unwilling to let Lew's attitude mess with the rest of her evening, Bonnie shifted Gunner's weight again as she walked across the parking lot.

It was the middle of August in Clearwater, Texas. No wonder sweat was already rolling down Bonnie's back. She couldn't wait until fall weather arrived, although they probably had at least another month or two before that happened.

Bonnie stepped onto the walkway that led to Joyful Hope

Stables. The moment a horse's whinny drifted to their ears, Gunner started bouncing up and down in her arms.

"Horsies! Go see horsies!"

Bonnie chuckled. "Yes, we're going to see the horses." She set him on his feet and quickly captured his chubby little hand in her own before he could run away from her.

Even with a busy toddler to keep track of, Bonnie instantly relaxed as the sounds of the horses and smell of hay and grass enveloped her. The stables, owned by her brother, Wyatt, and his wife, Chrissy, were one of her favorite places to be. She volunteered to help with hippotherapy sessions most Saturdays and tried to stop by to say hi once in a while. This time, though, she just wanted to get out of the house for a few minutes. She and Gunner were both going stir-crazy.

Bonnie found a spot to sit in the observation area and pulled some of Gunner's highly-prized toys from the backpack. They could watch from here for a little while until Gunner was no longer content and then she'd head back to her employer's home.

She loved watching these hippotherapy sessions. It was amazing how working with a horse helped everyone ranging from children with special needs to senior citizens. It wasn't just the way the horses connected with their riders, it was also how the actual act of riding the horse helped build core muscle strength, not to mention the rider's self-confidence.

Her attention zeroed in on a young boy with braces on his legs. Bonnie didn't know what made the braces necessary, but there was no missing the pure joy on the boy's face as he rode around gracefully. The faster the horse went, the wider the boy's smile.

Gunner held a tractor in one hand while he pointed to the horses with the other. "Go ride."

"You can't ride them, buddy. There's a class right now. Besides, I'd have to clear it with your daddy first." She'd never brought Gunner to ride but wondered whether Jace would object.

The boy looked like he was about to fuss about it but sat back down on the ground where he proceeded to push some dirt around with his toy.

A shadow fell over both of them, and Bonnie looked up to find her big brother smiling at her, one eyebrow raised.

"What are you doing here? Chrissy said you had a hot date tonight or something."

Bonnie rolled her eyes. Since Wyatt and Chrissy had married a year ago, Bonnie and Chrissy had become close. While Wyatt was still her best friend, Bonnie didn't often talk about dating or her boyfriends with him. That's what Chrissy was for. Of course, she expected the two of them to share notes.

She stood so she could visit with her brother easier but still keep an eye on Gunner. "I had to work late because Jace had an unexpected meeting tonight. I got an earful from Lew, which certainly didn't make my evening brighter. Anyway, Gunner and I were sick of sitting around the house. I hope it's okay that we dropped by for a few minutes."

Wyatt smiled at her. "Of course! It's always good to see you, and you're welcome any time." He regarded her with a measure of concern. "You work a lot of hours, Bonnie. If you have something else planned, it's okay to tell Jace no." He paused. "I hope Lew was at least respectful. He's left you hanging enough times that he doesn't have the right to complain when you have to cancel."

Wyatt had made it clear that he didn't care for Lew. As for Jace, Wyatt had only met him once, and it was in passing. He couldn't understand how hard it was to tell the man no, especially when he offered to pay time and a half in those instances. "It's okay. It sounds like the meeting was important."

"That might be, but your life is important, too."

Jace may be a director at some fancy financial institution his family owned, but Bonnie often thought he would've excelled in the Army as a drill sergeant.

It looked like Wyatt was going to object again. Bonnie held up a hand to stop him. "The rent on my place is going up three hundred after next month. I could use the extra money."

Wyatt's jaw dropped. "Three hundred? That's insane. You going to be okay?"

Bonnie appreciated his concern. If anyone knew of her financial situation, it was Wyatt. After all, they'd both chosen to walk away from the family fortune when they didn't conform to who their parents wanted them to be. Thankfully, she'd also understood the importance of saving money. The increase in rent was going to hurt, no doubt about it. Especially when she needed to sign a new lease next week. But she had a savings account, and the extra work hours lately did help.

"I'll be fine. I wish I could find a cheaper place to live, but moving on its own is expensive enough." She paused. "Jace is a good man to work for, Wyatt. The last-minute meetings get to me sometimes, but he pays me well." She looked down at Gunner with a smile. "And I do love this little guy." She glanced up again. "Don't worry, I have a ton of love reserved for my niece or nephew. How's Chrissy feeling?"

Wyatt's face morphed into a combination of pride, anticipation, and worry. He and Chrissy had announced they were expecting a baby a month ago. Poor Chrissy had been dealing with bouts of morning sickness that had her staying home and hugging the toilet more often than not. "She's exhausted. When I left to come here, she was asleep."

"I'll make a big batch of my chicken noodle soup and bring some over this weekend."

Wyatt grinned. "That would be great, thank you." His expression sobered again. "If you need to hit the batting cages, let me know."

That brought a smile to Bonnie's face. For years, if either of them needed to talk about something serious, they'd hit balls at the batting cage together. Bonnie had certainly worked out several problems with the help of her big brother and the satisfying sound of baseballs flying through the air. "I appreciate it, but I'm okay. I'll let you know if anything changes, though."

Wyatt nodded once and hitched a thumb behind him. "I'd better get going. Don't work too hard, okay?" He kissed her on the cheek. "Bye, Bon."

Bonnie waved at him while simultaneously snagging Gunner as he tried to escape and run toward the horses. "Don't even think about it, mister." As soon as he was in her arms, he arched his back and squealed.

Yep, their little outing was just about over. As much as she'd like to stay out for a while, it was time to get Gunner back. Besides, who knew how long it would be before Jace's meeting ended and he returned home? He would expect his son to be ready for bed when he did, though.

JACE ECHOLLS GLANCED ACROSS THE TABLE AT HIS TWIN sister, Noel, searching for confirmation that they'd heard the family's lawyer correctly. Noel blinked at him, clearly attempting to digest the information herself.

Their father, Shawn, hit the conference table with his palm while their mother, Leslie, bolted to her feet. "This is outrageous! There has to be some kind of mistake."

Mr. Lawson straightened the papers on the table in front of him, a picture of calm. He'd been employed by the Echolls family for many years and was used to the dramatics that always accompanied gatherings of any kind. "I assure you that everything is legal and binding just as I read it."

When his father had called Jace late that afternoon to insist on a reading of Grandpa's will, Jace had been annoyed at the lack of notice. There was no way his parents hadn't had the reading set up before then. But that's how they worked—making people bend to their timetables. He was surprised Grandpa had dared to die without consulting them first.

Then again, Grandpa always had been his own person. Something Jace greatly admired. When Jace looked at the man Grandpa had been, it was hard to believe that his own father was even related to him.

All through their childhood, his parents had sent him and Noel to live with Grandpa and Grandma for the summer while they traveled the world. To his parents, having children with them would be a huge inconvenience.

To Noel and Jace, summers on the ranch were anticipated all year long. All of Jace's favorite memories were linked to those months in one way or another. In many ways, his grandparents had given him and his sister the kind of love and attention they craved but never received from their own parents.

Still, to discover that the family ranch had been left completely to him and Noel was a shock. He'd fully expected it to be passed down to his father instead.

Apparently, his parents had expected it, too.

Father reached for a copy of the will that the lawyer passed to him and read it completely before looking up again. "The land that ranch is on has to be worth a small fortune to developers. It should've been signed over to me. I had plans to sell it as soon as the deed changed hands."

The very idea that Father would sell Grandpa's ranch had Jace's stomach lurching. Their grandparents loved that land.

They'd built the house and barn themselves and then had worked it together until Grandma passed away eight years ago. After that, Grandpa continued to stay there and work until his unexpected heart attack several weeks ago. A good friend of his was overseeing the place while its future was being decided.

Now that future was in Jace and Noel's hands. He had a lot to consider, but one thing was certain: He was not going to sell the land to some developer.

Noel clasped her long, blonde hair into a ponytail at the back of her neck, her blue eyes seeking his for answers and reassurance. Noel had dealt with anxiety for years, and this wasn't helping. Grandpa's farm had been a place of refuge for her, and he knew she didn't want to see it sold anymore than he did.

Their parents argued with each other about how the situation should be handled. "It's only fair that the land be sold. Your father and I should get half, and you two would split the other half," Mother insisted.

Jace ought to be shocked she wanted half to go to them, while he and Noel would each get twenty-five percent. Especially when the place had been left to them. But he wasn't, because that was who their mother was. Next to her, their father nodded in agreement.

Noel dropped her hair and clasped her hands in front of her as she took deep breaths. For her health as well as his sanity, Jace wasn't about to let this continue.

He cleared his throat and spoke, his deep voice projecting through the room. "The ranch will not be sold right now."

Both of his parents quieted immediately and looked at him as though he'd grown a third eye right in the middle of his head. "You can't be serious, son," Father said, his voice low but tinged with warning. "There's a great deal of money to be had there."

As if their parents needed more money. Sometimes Jace imagined his Father like Scrooge McDuck, with a whole room full of money that he swam through each night just to make himself feel better about life.

"I am completely serious. Noel and I spent a great deal of time out there, and we won't have its future decided on a whim. We have a lot to talk about and consider. When we've made our decision, we'll let you know."

Noel smiled at him from across the table and the panic on her face eased.

Mother started to say something, but Mr. Lawson straightened a stack of papers loudly. "Very well. I'll need the two of you to come by my office to sign some papers so the deed can be transferred to you." He stood and handed some paperwork to each of them. "I am, of course, available should you have any questions."

Jace accepted his with a nod. "Thank you. We'll call and set up an appointment." He intended to read through everything once he got home.

Mr. Lawson returned to his chair. "I believe that's the last of the business I needed to discuss with you all. Again, I'm sorry for your loss. I'm saddened that Jethro is no longer with us, but take solace knowing that he is once again sitting with Annie on Heaven's front porch. It has been an honor and a blessing to work for them all of these years." He packed the rest of the papers into his briefcase, closed it with a snap, and stood. "If you'll excuse me…" With that, he strode from the room.

The moment Mr. Lawson was gone, Father and Mother were on their feet. Jace knew they'd argue until the sun came up, and he wasn't in the mood to listen to it. He needed to get home to Gunner. Besides, he'd already asked Bonnie to stay longer than she was supposed to work today. Jace glanced at his watch and frowned. She was going to give him an earful when he got home.

"If you'll excuse me, I need to get back and put Gunner to bed." Truthfully, it was late enough that Bonnie was probably getting him down for the night right now. A pang of guilt hit him. He hadn't seen his son at all today.

At the mention of Gunner, Jace's father scowled. "I'm sure the nanny can manage that task."

Jace shot him a firm look. "It's been a long day." He walked around the table and put a hand protectively to his sister's back as he escorted her toward the door. He wasn't going to leave her in here to deal with the wolves. "Noel and I will let you know our decision about the ranch. Good night."

They made it out, down the hall, and into the elevator. As soon as the doors slid closed, Noel let herself slump against one wall as air whooshed from her lungs. "That was a nightmare. Thanks for the escape, big brother."

Her term of endearment brought a small smile to his face. He'd been born a mere two minutes before her, but he'd always clung to that and teased her about it when they were kids. "Not a problem. I suggest you put your phone on silent and don't answer their calls tonight or you'll never get any peace."

Noel nodded and proceeded to do exactly that. "I can't believe they want to just sell the ranch to make a profit." She swallowed hard. "The house and memories there are priceless."

"I agree. I need to get home, but I'll call you about it once I check on Gunner." There was no way he was going to be able to sleep anytime soon, and he suspected the same would be true for Noel.

"That sounds good."

Jace made sure she got to her car okay before getting into his own and starting the engine.

It was hard to believe Grandpa was gone. He'd left the ranch to them for a reason, and Jace sure wasn't going to let him down.

His thoughts shifted to Gunner. He wished he'd taken his son to the ranch more often than he had. It saddened him that Gunner wouldn't have his own memories of the place, or of his great grandfather.

At least Jace had plenty of stories to tell him when he got a little older.

He glanced at the clock and imagined Bonnie bathing his son and readying him for bed. At least he never had to worry about Gunner's well-being. He had no doubt Bonnie cared for him as she would her own child.

His heart flip-flopped as it often did when he thought about Bonnie. Seeing them together always had the same effect. He'd dealt with his fair share of guilt over it, too.

Truthfully, while he'd cared for Samantha and even loved her, they'd never been in love. She was a childhood friend who'd grown up in the foster care system. When she aged out, she struggled to make ends meet and work her way through college.

Their decision to get married meant financial stability for her and someone for him to spend life with. Gunner had been a surprise—but not an unwelcome one.

Unfortunately, marriage had brought out many of the little differences between him and Samantha, and they argued frequently. It didn't help that not only did his parents disap-prove of the marriage, but they were wholly unkind to Samantha.

Their marriage may not have been perfect, but they'd both wanted Gunner more than anything. And while

Samantha only had three days to love Gunner after he was born, she'd done so with all of her heart.

Now, Gunner was growing up without a mom, and he deserved better than that. Goodness knew Jace wasn't doing a fabulous job as an only parent. It was Bonnie who stood in the gap.

When he'd first hired her, she was only a constant reminder of the mom Gunner didn't have, and what Jace couldn't handle on his own. He'd put guidelines and strict rules in place so that Bonnie knew she was only supposed to focus on Gunner. That was it.

And then a year ago, his feelings for her softened. He began to see how much she truly cared for his son. Not only that, but she was kind, intelligent, and certainly had the patience of a saint to deal with him.

All qualities that had him frequently playing the "what if" game.

What if he'd met Bonnie years ago? What if she weren't his son's nanny? What if situations were different and he was allowed to care about Bonnie the way his heart told him he could?

As he had for the last year, he quickly slammed the door and turned the key on those emotions. He was neck-deep in his father's company and had a son to raise. He didn't have the luxury of playing games with his heart—or Gunner's.

Bonnie was his employee and vital to his son's well-being and happiness. Jace had no intention of risking that over some misplaced emotional reaction to her.

Period.

Chapter Two

onnie gave Gunner a bath, got him his milk, and even tossed a load of the toddler's laundry into the washing machine. She'd always done Gunner's laundry, but not once had she done Jace's. He'd been clear when he first hired her that her household duties would be strictly restricted to things that related to Gunner and nothing else.

In the beginning, she'd done more than he'd listed, especially in the evenings when she'd watched over Gunner after he'd gone to sleep. At the time, she knew his wife had passed away and could only imagine how hard things were on him. He never spoke about it, but at least it was one way Bonnie could help.

Jace had reprimanded her and insisted she only do the jobs that were outlined when he hired her. It wasn't that big of a deal to Bonnie, but it was just another example of how he kept a wall between personal life and work.

She got it, truly, she did. Maybe she just didn't have as much of a personal life to go home to as Jace did. She thought about Lew and groaned. Yeah, even when she considered her boyfriend. Truthfully, they hadn't been getting along all that great the last few months. She'd thought about breaking things off with him, except she hadn't seen him long enough to do so between his crazy schedule and hers.

Late work nights like tonight certainly didn't help her in the personal life department.

It was nearing nine o'clock, and she was ready for Jace to get home already and then she could do the same. Irritation flared.

She flopped onto the plush couch with a sigh. Why couldn't Jace get that she had a life to get back to, too?

Thoughts about the ruined date, Lew's bad attitude, plus Wyatt's comments about her working too much combined until Bonnie tapped her foot to the rhythm of the slow-moving clock on the wall. What she wanted was to go home, curl up on the couch with a bowl of ice cream, and watch reruns of a favorite television show.

Gunner had been asleep for an hour now. Bonnie wasn't about to sit on the couch and mope. Instead, she finished folding Gunner's laundry and placed it on the dresser in his room before deciding to check on the little boy again. He was passed out in his toddler bed, his hands behind his head in a look of pure innocence and relaxation.

She reached out and ran a finger across his cheek as a wave of love crashed into her heart. She might be annoyed with Jace for often working late but caring for Gunner was never a burden.

With a final look at him, she left the room, closing the door softly behind her.

The moment she stepped off the last stair onto the first floor, the front door of the large home opened. The annoyance from earlier rose again as Jace walked in dressed in a suit and tie like he wore every day. She suppressed the biting words forming on her tongue and watched as he dropped a briefcase onto a nearby table before turning to look at her.

Those bright blue eyes had her pulse thrumming in her

ears. He ran his fingers through his short-cropped, dark blond hair—hair that never seemed to be out of place. He couldn't be more than two or three inches taller than Bonnie, but his ability to command the room made him appear much larger than life.

A muscle twitched in his strong jaw as a shadow of regret crossed his features. "I didn't intend to be back this late. The meeting ran much longer than I anticipated." His gaze went from her to the staircase as he loosened the tie around his neck. "How's Gunner?"

"He's fast asleep. We had a good day." The exhausted look on Jace's face brought Bonnie's annoyance down a notch or two. "He was a little fussier than normal. I'm wondering if his two-year molars are starting to come in."

Jace's expression remained neutral. "I hate that I didn't get to see him today." He paused. "I hope the change in plans wasn't an inconvenience."

Bonnie considered giving him the polite, "Of course not." But Wyatt was right, she'd been working too much lately. Jace took for granted that she'd be able to simply adjust her schedule to meet his needs. She rolled her shoulders back. "I had a date with my boyfriend that I had to cancel last minute."

His eyes widened slightly. "I didn't realize. I apologize. I hope you blamed the cancellation on me and my schedule."

"Oh, I did. He wasn't exactly understanding." Okay, that was more information than she'd planned on sharing, even if it was true. Her cheeks warmed, and she covered the reaction by retrieving her shoulder bag. "I'm sure a meeting that ran this late couldn't have been much fun." She wasn't sure why she said that last bit. Small talk wasn't their thing. Usually, she relayed the day's events to him, he reminded her of any changes in the coming week or two, and she took her leave.

If Jace thought much of her question, he didn't show it.

"It proved to be even more unpleasant—and surprising—than I anticipated." He covered a yawn.

"Well, I hope you get some time to relax tonight. You and Gunner have a good weekend." She meant that. "I'll see you on Monday." She raised a hand in farewell and walked past him to the door.

"Bonnie?"

She stopped and turned, unaware that he'd followed her and how closely he was standing now. She had to take a step back so she could look up at him. Instantly, the subtle scent of something woodsy surrounded her. It was a scent that often lingered after he left for work, and one she'd always liked. Just because of the scent itself, of course, not because of the man who wore it. No guy should smell that good after working all day.

Bonnie assumed Jace wanted an update on how the rest of their evening had gone. "Oh! Yes, I did finish Gunner's laundry. I put everything on top of the dresser, I didn't want to risk waking him up by putting it away. I can do that Monday if you don't get to it over the weekend."

Jace held up a hand to stop her. "I only wanted to say thank you, and that I hope you have a good weekend as well."

"I appreciate it." Bonnie hurried out before her cheeks got any pinker. The door closed securely behind her.

Her employer's unusual chattiness—at least for him—had Bonnie wondering what might have happened at the meeting. Not for the first time, Bonnie wished she knew more about him outside of what she had to know as his employee.

She was finally off work. As usual on Friday evenings, Bonnie walked to her car looking forward to the weekend off but knowing full well that she'd be missing Gunner—and his dad—by the middle of Saturday.

ᥫ᭡

JACE STOOD AT THE WINDOW AND WATCHED BONNIE UNTIL she was safely in her car and pulling away from his house. He'd regretted asking her to work late. Of course she had other things to do, but he'd never considered she might be seeing someone.

And why shouldn't she? Truthfully, Jace often marveled that she wasn't already married. Not only was she amazing with kids—his in particular—but she was kind and incredibly patient. She had to be to put up with his crazy work schedule. Oh, she definitely let him know when she didn't appreciate his late evenings. In fact, her candor was something he appreciated, even if it did mean they butted heads on a semi-regular basis.

Bonnie was also drop-dead gorgeous. He reminded himself that last observation was one any sane man would make. He'd worried on more than one occasion about what he would do should she ever decide to quit working for him. It was always one of those hypothetical worries until now.

She was dating someone. There was a man out there somewhere who was lucky enough to call himself Bonnie's boyfriend. The guy would be crazy if he didn't eventually put a ring on the woman's finger before she got away.

Which meant his concern that Bonnie might one day move on suddenly became very real.

Jace frowned.

If he were ever in a position to fight for her to continue working for him, getting home this late and causing her to cancel her date wouldn't help his case. How many other things had she canceled because of his schedule?

He'd half expected her to snap at him tonight—it wouldn't be the first time. She'd apparently thought about it, too, but the annoyance on her face hadn't lasted long. At one point, those pretty dark brown eyes of hers had shed their frustration and taken on a sheen of concern resulting in a spark of warmth that radiated throughout his chest.

Every time he looked into her eyes, they threatened to pull him in. And her smile... It would be so easy to care about her more than he should.

There were times he wondered what it would be like if he got to know her better. Even allow a friendship to develop. Being friends with her would never be dull.

A grin tugged at the corners of his mouth.

No.

He needed a nanny for his son. Preferably someone stable who would be with them until Gunner was at least in kindergarten. That meant lines needed to be drawn and strictly adhered to.

It was better this way.

He needed something else to focus his thoughts on, and the ranch issues were just the ticket. He pulled his phone out and dialed Noel's number.

She answered in moments. "Hey, Jace. Long time, no talk."

Jace chuckled. "Right?" His stomach rumbled, reminding him that he hadn't eaten a thing since lunch. He headed for the kitchen. "You make it home okay?" He grabbed a pocket sandwich out of the freezer, placed it on a plate, and popped it into the microwave.

"I did. I'm glad I followed your advice and turned the ringer off on my phone. While I waited for you, Mom and Dad called me three times." Her voice betrayed her exhaustion. "How's Gunner?"

"He's fast asleep upstairs." Their parents had better not continue to harass Noel or he was going to have to give them a piece of his mind. He and Noel needed to decide what to do with the ranch sooner than later. At least once they made an official announcement, it might get their parents off their backs. Maybe.

Jace retrieved his food and collapsed onto the couch in the living room. He kicked his shoes off and rested his feet on the coffee table. Noel loved to formulate plans for everything—it was one way she was able to relieve some of her anxiety. "So what are your thoughts about the ranch?"

He imagined Noel sitting cross-legged, her planner open on her lap, and a notebook nearby. She'd have a list of ideas with details as to why each one was an option.

Noel didn't hesitate. "I think you and Gunner should move to the ranch and you should run it yourself."

Jace had taken a large bite of his food and nearly choked. "You're kidding. I can't run a ranch."

"Why not?"

That was all Noel had to offer? She must not have had time to add bullet points to her idea. It wasn't nearly enough for Jace. "You're going to have to do a little more to convince me." He took another bite of the sandwich.

"You were out there every summer helping Grandpa, and you loved every minute of it. Remember when you used to want to be a rancher just like him?"

Yeah, he did. Back when life was a little simpler than it was now. He tried to focus on Noel's voice as she continued to speak.

"There would be a learning curve just like anything, but it would be perfect. You're always complaining about your job and how much overtime it requires. Not to mention wearing a suit all the time."

He hadn't realized he'd complained about his job that much. It definitely did consume a lot of time—time that took him away from Gunner. He added that to the list of regrets that grew longer by the minute tonight.

But run his grandfather's ranch? Not only would that be

taking a huge pay cut, but there's no way he could take care of everything around a ranch with Gunner in tow. He told Noel as much. "Unless, of course, you moved out there with me." He was mostly joking because he couldn't imagine Noel doing such a thing.

Her contemplative silence surprised him. She finally took a deep breath. "I can't quit my job. I need it for the insurance." She paused. "But getting away from town and out of my horrible apartment would be nice. I could help you with Gunner."

Jace was so thrown by Noel's response that it took several moments to form words. If Noel moved in, she could watch Gunner on the weekends when he needed to check on things around the ranch. But what about the weekdays? "I doubt Bonnie would be willing to drive out there every day."

Noel's answer came quickly. "She could take the apartment above the garage. We might have to clean it up some, but it's beautiful out there. It'd only be for another few years until Gunner was in school."

This was absolutely insane. To go from a high-paying job like the one he had now to running a sheep ranch?

It wasn't the money. He had a substantial savings account and the interest to live off of. It was more the responsibility of taking over the ranch his grandparents built from the ground up and loved for many years.

What if he failed to keep it running?

Noel's voice interrupted his thoughts as it filtered through the phone. "The ranch is our responsibility now. I don't know about you, but I don't want to sell the land. Can we trust someone else to keep it running for us?"

Grandpa employed several men who lived and worked on the property to help him. But he always managed the ranch himself and kept a tight rein on anything that happened under his watch. No, Grandpa wouldn't have wanted a stranger to run it. In fact, Jace was certain his grandfather would prefer they sell the land as opposed to hiring someone else to work it.

He always did say working on the ranch built character, and that the world would be a better place if more people worked with their hands.

"No, he would've hated that." Which left them with little choice.

Which would Jace regret more? Selling his grandfather's ranch or walking away from his life the way it was now to run it?

The answer was easy. He shook his head, hardly able to believe this was happening.

"We both need to be praying about it, Noel, but I'm not entirely opposed to your idea. We have a lot to address before we make a decision, though."

He and Noel started throwing topics, roadblocks, and ideas out as they talked through the true logistics of it all.

Meanwhile, in the back of his mind, he wondered whether Bonnie would even consider moving into the apartment above the garage and continue to work as Gunner's nanny.

His mind went to the guy she was supposed to go out with tonight. Would her boyfriend like the idea of Bonnie moving onto a ranch?

He thought about the two of them cuddling on the couch as they talked about the option. A wave of jealousy crashed into him that he had no right to feel. If the roles were reversed, Jace knew he wouldn't want his girlfriend going to live with some rancher he didn't know just outside of town.

Still, she obviously loved working with Gunner. Jace couldn't fathom hiring anyone else. On one hand, it would be a huge help to have Bonnie so close. On the other, living on the same property would blur some of those lines he'd worked hard to put in place.

He and Noel agreed to pray about it before ending their phone call.

That's exactly what Jace planned to do, but he was already experiencing more peace about this possibility than he had anything in a long time.

"If this is truly what You want me to do, God, I'm going to need some help getting things lined up." That included providing another nanny for Gunner or convincing Bonnie to move to the ranch with him.

Jace was definitely hoping for the latter.

Chapter Three

Bonnie stifled a yawn Monday morning as she retrieved her bag from the passenger seat of her car and got out. It was time to start a new week at the Echolls home, and while she could've used more sleep, she looked forward to seeing little Gunner.

Normally, she would knock on the door and wait for Jace to answer dressed in his usual slacks, newly-pressed shirt, and jacket. He'd usher her in, give her any instructions he might have for the day, and then promptly grab his briefcase before leaving for work.

It'd been like that nearly every day since she'd been hired.

Until today.

Jace opened the door, sans jacket, one hand holding his cell phone to his ear. He motioned for her to enter as he spoke to someone on the other end of the phone conversation. "Of course. Whatever we need to do to get the house on the market as soon as possible."

Bonnie shouldn't listen in on Jace's conversation, but it was impossible not to given he was standing right in front of her.

They spoke about house inspections and furniture staging for showings. Which house was Jace talking about selling? Surely not this one, because that could mean—

Jace thanked the other person and ended the phone call. He offered Bonnie a sympathetic look. "I'm sorry about that. As you probably heard, I'm putting this house on the market."

Bonnie's heart fell to her feet. Jace and Gunner were moving? She'd contemplated a lot of situations over the years where she might lose her job as Gunner's nanny. Most of the time, it was because she argued with Jace over something and got herself fired. She hadn't considered they might move. The idea of not seeing Gunner regularly—much less at all—had her heart aching more than she'd thought possible.

Her mind tried to grasp what all of this meant.

She'd need another job and fast, especially with rent going up. She made a mental note to reach out to the nanny group she was a member of and peruse the job listings. What if she couldn't find another position right away?

Jace said something else that had her thoughts crashing to a halt.

She blinked at him. "Wait, what?"

"I would like you to continue to be Gunner's nanny. I know it would be a lot to ask you to drive to the new location every day, and I wouldn't expect you to do that. Instead, there's a furnished apartment above the garage that would be yours." Jace was all business, down to the tone of his voice. He'd clearly thought everything through.

Which gave him an advantage. The last thing Bonnie expected when she arrived at his house on this Monday morning was to find her job was going to change. Was this no-nonsense approach how he handled his business meetings every day? Probably.

He wanted her to move into an apartment above the

garage? How much would he charge for rent? She pictured rickety stairs leading up from a dirty garage to a place that always smelled of gas and motor oil. Where was this ranch located? If they were going to be secluded miles from civilization—just the three of them—Bonnie wasn't sure that was such a good idea.

There would be no escaping Jace at the end of the day. At least not completely.

The myriad of doubts she entertained must have shown clearly on her face. Jace watched her closely. "I don't expect you to accept without seeing the ranch or the apartment." He glanced at his watch. "If your schedule permits, we could drive out there this morning and I could show you around. That way you can make an informed decision."

Bonnie's eyes widened. She couldn't recall a time Jace had stayed home from work. Not even when he came down with a cold. Her mouth opened and closed again.

He was watching her with those gorgeous blue eyes, clearly waiting for her response. His poker face was firmly in place, making it impossible for her to decipher what he might be thinking. One thing was certain, though. He was right— she needed to see the ranch and apartment before she could possibly give Jace an answer.

It was barely seven in the morning. She thought of Gunner asleep upstairs. "Gunner should be waking soon. I need to make him some breakfast and pack a few things in his backpack. We should be able to leave after that."

Jace gave a definitive nod, a flash of approval in his eyes. "That sounds good. I'll be in my office. Let's plan to leave by eight-thirty."

"That will give me plenty of time," Bonnie agreed. She watched him disappear down the hallway.

Normally, when she arrived for work, Jace was on his way out of the house. Other than providing a few requests or directions, they spoke very little. She was then left to care for Gunner and everything else on her own. Sometimes the days got long, but she was used to it. She knew where everything was and felt at home there.

Normally, anyway.

Knowing Jace was in the house somewhere while she picked things up and prepared breakfast was more than a little weird.

Was that an indication she should turn down Jace's idea of moving to the ranch?

Bonnie took a deep breath. She would need time to consider everything. Talk to Wyatt and Chrissy to get their opinion. Praying definitely wouldn't hurt. "I'm going to need a little nudge from You as we go through today. A blatant 'yes' or 'no' would be great, too."

Bonnie set her bag down by the front door, grabbed the baby monitor from a nearby table, and proceeded to go upstairs to the little boy's room.

He was still asleep, even though he shifted a little as she entered. He would be up and going soon. Bonnie took advantage of the time she had to add a few toys, diapers, and some other supplies to his backpack.

Meanwhile, her mind kept wandering to this ranch that she'd agreed to go see. It didn't mean she was committing to anything. She was just gathering all the facts, something Wyatt would agree with wholeheartedly.

Would she seriously consider moving in order to keep her job as Gunner's nanny? When would Jace expect an answer from her? He likely needed one as soon as possible, and she couldn't blame him. If she said no to the change in her job, he'd need to start a search for a new nanny.

The idea that someone else could potentially be caring for Gunner brought with it a pang of loneliness. She'd known her job was likely to only last until he started kindergarten. But at least that was still a few years down the road.

Bonnie was fortunate to have worked for Jace for two years. Losing her job or having to find a new family to nanny for was a possibility she always knew existed, even if she hadn't had to deal with it.

She still didn't. Not really, because nothing had changed.

Yet.

Bonnie looked over to find Gunner scrambling down from his toddler bed and running across the room for her to pick him up.

The little boy was so active lately, that the only time she got any cuddles in was first thing in the morning and right before she put him down for bed on the nights Jace worked late.

She scooped him into her arms and moved to the rocking chair. Gunner snuggled against her chest.

"We're going on an adventure today. Your daddy is home, and he's going to take us to go look at a ranch. Would you like that?"

"See horses."

"I'm not sure what we'll see." Now that he mentioned it, Bonnie hadn't thought to ask what kind of ranch it was. "But it'll be a lot of fun. We'd better get you downstairs to eat breakfast and then get dressed. Do you want a pancake?"

Gunner nodded, climbed down from her lap, and ran for his bedroom door.

And her busy day began—except she would be spending time not only with her young charge, but with his handsome father as well.

That last thought sent a wave of nervous flutters through her stomach.

❧

It was surreal to be sitting in the passenger seat of Jace's brand new Ford F-150. It wasn't the first vehicle Bonnie thought of when it came to her wealthy employer. In fact, that's exactly what set him apart from the other rich individuals she knew.

Take her own parents, for instance. They often drove their Mercedes while the Tesla remained in the garage to prevent them from being damaged.

As for Bonnie, she much preferred something more practical. Or at least vehicles that didn't cost as much as a house.

Gunner gave a surprised gasp from the back seat. "Cow!"

Jace chuckled. "It sure is, big guy. There are a lot of cows out here. Do you remember Great Grandpa's ranch and all of the sheep?"

There was a tinge of sadness in his voice that had Bonnie's heart aching for him.

"Baaa!" Gunner announced from his seat.

Bonnie half turned to give him a smile. When she faced forward again, she addressed Jace. "A sheep ranch. How interesting. Will you be helping your grandpa?"

Jace cleared his throat and didn't respond for several seconds. "Grandpa passed a few weeks ago. He left the place to my sister and me. We've decided to do our best to keep it running."

Why hadn't he told her that this morning when he mentioned moving to a ranch? Or say something when his grandpa passed away in the first place? There was no missing the emotion in his voice. They must have been close. "I'm sorry for your loss." She paused. "I lost my grandpa some years ago, but I still have Gran, praise God. Grandparents are important."

"Yes, they are." There was something in his voice that hinted at nostalgia.

Bonnie wanted to ask him more but knew he wouldn't

welcome the questions. "Gunner is lucky to have met his great grandpa. Raising him on the ranch your grandpa probably cared a great deal about would surely make him happy."

Jace glanced at her, a mixture of surprise, warmth, and sadness in his blue eyes. "I think it would, too." He cleared his throat again. "We're only a few minutes from our exit. As you can see, it's not that far from Clearwater. But between the narrow roads and the distance, the less you have to drive back and forth in the dark the better."

She'd certainly done plenty of driving home at night in the past, especially in the winter, though it wasn't nearly this far. His concern warmed her.

Since Jace would be working on the ranch, surely he wouldn't be nearly as late returning home as he ran now.

"It's pretty out here." The trees parted to reveal a large field dotted with sheep grazing lazily. "Are they yours?"

Jace's spine straightened as he gave a single nod. "Yup. We have four hundred."

"Wow." Most of the sheep were white with black heads. "What are they raised for?"

"Meat and leather." He looked at her again, obviously expecting her to object. "These particular sheep are hairless Dorper. They are highly adaptable, tolerant of the heat, resistant to parasites, and are low maintenance." A small smile tugged at the corners of his lips. "At least according to Grandpa."

"Do you have experience working with sheep? Or will this all be new to you?"

"Noel and I stayed with Grandpa every summer through our childhood. We learned a lot about it then, but it's been a while."

"Noel is your sister?"

"Yes. My twin."

Bonnie's mind reeled. She'd learned more about her

employer in the last thirty minutes than she had since she'd started working for him. She remembered hearing he had a sister but had no idea what her name was or that she was his twin.

Why did his parents send the kids away each summer? It was impossible not to draw on her own experience. She and her siblings had been enrolled in back-to-back activities that a driver took them to. If possible, they were busier during the summer than they were the school year. There were certainly no family activities or vacations to speak of.

"My situation was different, but the times we got to spend with my grandparents were some of my favorite."

Jace nodded. "Mine, too." He remained silent as they turned onto a side road that turned into a long driveway.

Gunner chatted behind them as the ranch house came into view.

Bonnie wasn't sure what she expected, but this wasn't it. She'd gone back and forth between imagining something akin to a castle and a rickety little log cabin.

This was somewhere in between. Elegant. It was positively beautiful with a wrap-around porch that went across the front and down one side, white paint, and blue accents and shutters.

"This is amazing. Whoever designed it had some serious talent."

"My grandparents designed it themselves." Jace pulled onto the large circular driveway in front of the house. "Thank you. If Grandpa were here, he would humor you with stories of how he and Grandma argued over options, and how she won nearly every time." He stopped suddenly as though he hadn't meant to get so personal. Or maybe some of those memories were too painful to relive right now. "Come on, I'll give you a tour of the house, and then you can take a look at the garage and the apartment above it. Both are around behind the house itself."

Bonnie nodded her agreement. She couldn't see the garage past the two-story house.

Jace got out of the truck and was at Bonnie's door holding it open before she'd been able to get it herself.

As her feet touched the ground, the scent of the trees and land around her somehow mixed with the scent of Jace's aftershave. Oddly enough, the combination fit him perfectly.

She inhaled deeply before realizing she was just standing there, staring. Thankfully, he didn't seem to realize she was standing there thinking about the way he smelled. Probably a good thing.

Bonnie shook her head to clear her thoughts and moved to get Gunner out of the back seat. He nearly exploded with energy as he was released from the confines of the truck. The first thing the little boy did was run to a pile of gravel and proceed to chuck little rocks at the underpinning of the porch.

Since Jace didn't reprimand Gunner, neither did Bonnie. She didn't blame him for needing to get some energy worked off. Her attention again shifted to the large house in front of her.

The details made all the difference. Rose bushes were planted along most of the front of the house. She could tell there were sheer curtains hanging in the windows on the inside. There was even a porch swing that just begged for her to sit on it.

She could understand why Jace decided to move here.

Jace swung Gunner up onto his shoulders and led the way up the steps to the front door. He unlocked it and then allowed Bonnie to go in ahead of him.

The large picture windows let in sunlight rendering the lamps unnecessary. The living room was expansive, beautifully decorated with a plush couch and two recliners, and a wood-burning stove along one wall. Overladen bookshelves lined another. It would be easy for Bonnie to feel at home here.

"This is the living room," Jace announced unnecessarily. He walked through it and into the kitchen.

Bonnie found she had to move quickly to keep up as they toured the kitchen, dining room, study, and utility room downstairs as well as a large bedroom. "Noel will be staying here."

Bonnie wondered if Noel was going to be moving to the farm permanently as well, or if it was a temporary arrangement.

She liked the idea of having someone besides just the three of them out here. Hopefully, she and Noel would get along nicely.

Assuming, of course, Bonnie agreed to the job change in the first place.

After that, they headed upstairs. Bonnie allowed her hand to brush the wooden banister as she admired the multitude of family pictures that lined the wall all the way up to the second floor.

She paused at a photo of two young kids—a boy and a girl—smiling as they sat in a tree, legs dangling. They looked to be around ten years old. Even back then, Bonnie could tell the boy was Jace. He looked happy. Content.

Jace must have noticed her hesitation because he came back down the steps and stopped beside her. "We climbed that tree every summer. It's still standing out back." He smiled. "I bet Gunner will be climbing it before we know it."

No doubt that was true. Gunner wasn't afraid of heights.

Bonnie followed Jace upstairs as he showed her the master bedroom and adjoining bath, the bedroom that would be Gunner's, and another room that his grandparents had used as a craft room of sorts. Right now, it looked more like a cluttered storage room.

Her favorite spot in the whole house, however, was along one wall not far from the staircase landing. An alcove had been built into the wall and lined with windows. How had Jace's grandpa somehow glimpsed into the future and known Bonnie's heart? The perfect window seat had been added, begging her to bring her favorite book, a soft throw, and read until there was no more daylight.

As though her feet had a mind of their own, they led her to the alcove where she tried to guess which direction it was facing. It looked like it would be possible to watch the sunset from here. How perfect was that?

Footsteps behind her announced Jace's presence. "As you can see, the garage has been kept in excellent condition. I can assure you the apartment has as well." He pointed. "Beyond that, although you can't see it from here, is another barn and quarters where Cabe, Grandpa's good friend and the man keeping this place running right now, lives alone. We have two other men that drive in to handle the everyday chores."

Bonnie's eyes went from the horizon and her imagined sunset to the three-car garage that she saw behind the house. It was painted to match the house, and like Jace said, it looked immaculate.

Jace must have taken her silence for uncertainty. "Once you check out the apartment, if you agree to stay, you are welcome to decorate it any way you'd like."

He shifted, his arm just brushing hers, before moving away again. The touch sparked goosebumps that skittered across her skin and had her heart pounding in her ears. She forced herself to breathe normally.

Moving here would be a bad idea. It'd been easy enough to ignore her attraction to Jace when she rarely saw him. In fact, she'd thought those feelings had had disappeared a long time ago. She had a boyfriend now, and even thinking about Jace as anyone but her employer was a waste of time. A pang of guilt zapped her as her thoughts shifted to Lew. Oh, he'd hate she was even contemplating this move.

Her eyes again scanned the view before her. Peace filled her, and Bonnie didn't know if it was the stillness outside, the house itself, or a general contentment about her current situation. Either way, she knew, without seeing the apartment, that it was going to be nearly impossible to turn down Jace's offer.

Chapter Four

Jace wished he knew what Bonnie thought of the ranch. The house wasn't nearly as large or as fancy as his, but it still had a lot of charm and had been kept up beautifully by Grandma, and later by a housekeeper Grandpa hired.

Bonnie came from one of the wealthiest families in Clearwater—a fact he'd discovered some time ago when he'd run background checks on the woman who would be caring for his son. She'd never come off as someone fixated on money, though. She drove a normal car, dressed conservatively, and not once had she asked for a raise.

Truthfully, he'd admired all of that about her. It'd only solidified his decision to hire her back then, and it was one of many reasons why he hoped she'd agree to move with them now.

He watched as she continued to gaze through the alcove window. The sunlight had her dark hair shining as though there were little bits of glitter sprinkled throughout. It almost looked like silk, and for a fraction of a second, Jace wondered if it would be as soft.

He plunged his hands into his pockets. He wasn't

normally an overly sentimental man. But Grandpa's death and standing here in the house Jace wished he could've grown up in was enough to make anyone reminisce.

Had Grandma ever stood like Bonnie and watched as Grandpa came in from the barn after a long workday? How would it feel to know someone anticipated your return like that?

Bonnie looked like she belonged there, and he said a silent prayer that she'd agree to stay on as Gunner's nanny. If she chose not to, he'd find another, but it wouldn't be easy.

He wished he knew her better, then maybe he could make an educated guess about her answer.

Gunner, who had been content to explore the nearly-empty room that would be his bedroom, dashed out and toward the staircase. Jace caught him easily, but the motion snagged Bonnie's attention. She turned and grabbed Gunner's other little hand.

"Baby gates."

Jace and Bonnie said the words at precisely the same time, eliciting smiles from both of them.

Jace nodded. "First on my list." He had them at his house at the top and bottom of the stairs. With his adventurous son, they were more than necessary. "Are you ready to see the apartment?"

Bonnie's dark lashes lifted, and her gaze met his. "Sure." She hesitated. "Do you want me to take Gunner?" She glanced down at the boy. They were each still holding onto one of his hands.

Jace could understand her uncertainty since she was technically on the clock. At the same time, he rarely saw his son during the day. He lifted Gunner into his arms. "I've got the little rascal."

Jace tickled Gunner until the boy was giggling before leading the way back downstairs.

They went out the back door, across a wooden porch, and followed the paved path to the garage. In addition to the main garage doors, there was a side entrance protected from the weather by a roof that bridged the gap between the house and the garage. Jace liked that, when the weather got bad, Bonnie wouldn't have to be out in the elements to get from her apartment to the house to care for Gunner.

He noted the acre of land behind the house. Grandpa had kept the whole area mowed impeccably, and if the short grass were any indication, the men Grandpa hired were doing a good job of taking care of things in his absence. Soon, it would be his responsibility.

Jace pictured having play equipment installed for Gunner in the near future. His son would love that.

Bonnie pointed toward an old chicken coop. "Did your grandpa raise more than sheep?"

"He used to have chickens. He's had a cow or two in the past, but not now. Mostly, he would rent a few acres out to someone who wanted to keep some cattle but had no land themselves." Right now, the thought of caring for the sheep was more than enough for Jace. If things went well, maybe they could get a few chickens again in a year or so.

He pointed to the pasture on the right. "The sheep are probably at the stock tank—but some of them are in that pasture there."

"That's neat that sometimes you can see them from the house."

There was a hint of wonder mixed in with the interest in her voice. Enough to give Jace hope that maybe she would agree to move here with them. Especially since she appreciated the beauty of the ranch.

It was a shame his parents never had. He thought back to the conversation he had with them yesterday once he and Noel had officially decided to keep the ranch. Jace wasn't sure which of his parents had yelled louder. Eventually, he'd set his phone on the table until they'd calmed down. When it was clear Jace wasn't going to change his mind, his parents had hung up. He hadn't talked to them since.

He wished Noel were here today. It'd be good for Bonnie to meet her. Plus, having another woman around might help ease any of Bonnie's misgivings. "Do you have any questions for me?"

She appeared thoughtful as she fingered the hem of her blouse. There was something about the way one corner of her mouth tipped just a little as she thought that had him biting back a smile. She hesitated. "I do have one, and I'm just going to be blunt."

He motioned for her to continue. He admired that about her, even if it meant they didn't always agree. He'd much rather know how she felt and deal with a situation than all the speculation. Trying to guess what someone else does or doesn't want and then getting dinged for it was one of his pet peeves.

Bonnie fiddled with the hem another moment or two before dropping her arms. "I know things come up, and I don't mind working late occasionally, especially if it's arranged ahead of time." She cleared her throat. "Assuming we agreed to go forward with this, I would want to make sure we had a firm work schedule in place to prevent late evenings from happening too frequently."

Her posture suggested that she wished she didn't have to bring up the subject at all, but the intensity in her eyes told him she was quite serious.

He'd taken advantage of her willingness to stay late in the past and again regretted that. He raised a hand. "You are absolutely right. Noel won't leave until eight in the morning, and she will be home by six. If something does come up and I need to work late, she can take over watching Gunner at that point." He chuckled. "And yes, she and I have talked about this already. I'm fortunate that Gunner has such a devoted aunt."

That brought a smile to Bonnie's face. "It is great to have that support."

Jace didn't know what he would do without Noel. Or Bonnie. "If something does come up for either me or Noel that delays us, we'll do our best to let you know in advance."

Bonnie's cheeks turned a light shade of pink. Was she thinking about her boyfriend? Or was she embarrassed about their conversation on Friday night? He doubted the latter. He did hope her boyfriend had chosen to forgive her for canceling since it hadn't been her fault. Jace thought about asking but stopped himself, figuring it wasn't his business.

"That sounds fair," she said. "That was my main concern outside of the cost of rent for the apartment."

Jace stopped walking and turned to look at her. "Oh! I thought I'd mentioned before that it was included. Consider it a bonus."

Her mouth opened and closed again. "That's a huge bonus."

He laughed. It wasn't often that he found her at a loss for words. "The apartment is just sitting here empty. I'd rather have someone occupy the space and keep an eye on it. You would be doing me a favor."

Gunner ran ahead of them to the garage door and tried to get it open. Jace unlocked the door, waited for his son to twist the knob, and then held the door for Bonnie. Just inside the garage and to the right was a staircase. Jace motioned for Bonnie to go ahead of him.

"There's a second door that leads into the apartment, but it's usually unlocked. Of course, if you decide to stay here, you'll be given a key. This was originally built for my Grandma's mom, who happened to be picky about a great number of things."

Bonnie turned the knob and stepped into the apartment with a gasp. Jace's stomach fell to the floor. He should've come and looked at the place first. Who knows when Grandpa had last cleaned it?

Jace stepped through the doorway expecting to discover the place in shambles or reduced to more storage.

Instead, he found it was in perfect condition. Bonnie took it all in, appreciation on her face. "Are you serious? This looks more like some fancy room at a bed and breakfast than it does an apartment above a garage."

His shoulders relaxed. He closed the door behind them and set Gunner back down on the floor. Jace smiled at Bonnie, though she wasn't paying him any attention. "All furniture is included. But if you have your own, this can be moved into storage. There's a nice-sized kitchen and all appliances, including a washer and dryer. Everything you need to be self-sufficient."

Bonnie nodded thoughtfully. "It certainly is beautiful." She turned to look at him. "I have a guinea pig."

That was the last thing he expected her to say. "Okay." He fought back a smile. He tried to picture her sitting around an apartment holding a guinea pig and failed miserably.

"I thought I should mention it in case bringing her would be a problem."

"As long as she doesn't run loose, I don't have an issue with it." He wanted to ask her if it meant she was considering staying on as Gunner's nanny, but he didn't want to rush her.

Instead, he entertained Gunner while she took a complete look around the apartment. When she returned, Gunner ran up to her. She picked him up and settled him on her hip without a second thought.

"It's an amazing place. Nicer than my current apartment. And you're sure I don't need to pay rent?"

"One hundred percent." If she had another apartment, there may be fees required for her to get out of the lease. He mentioned as much, but she shook her head.

"I was about to sign a new lease next week. The timing is perfect." She quieted for several heartbeats. "And you're sure your sister won't mind my being here?"

"Not at all. Moving here was her idea in the first place, and she encouraged me to ask you as well." He offered her a smile. "Not having as many late evenings will be good for everyone."

As far as Jace's job went, everything would change drastically, and he had no idea what that really meant. Since Gunner was too young to go out with him, having Gunner—and Bonnie—so close would be a comfort. Maybe he could even drop by at lunch to check on them.

That would mean spending more time not only with Gunner but with Bonnie as well. A thought that was way more appealing than it should be. He bit back a groan.

Is it wrong, God, to pray that she'll give in and move here with us? Is it messed up that I'm just as nervous she'll say yes as I am that she might say no?

Bonnie's voice interrupted his thoughts. "Would it be okay if I let you know tomorrow?"

"Of course. Take several days if you need it. If you could let me know by the end of the week, I'd appreciate it." He'd need time to hire another nanny, something he didn't look forward to dealing with. "I apologize for the late notice. If it helps, I didn't know anything about this myself until Friday night." He gave her a reassuring smile. "Thank you for being willing to consider it."

If Bonnie took the apartment, it'd be a lot harder to keep different aspects of his life separate. Even still, if it meant keeping her employed and a part of their lives, the challenge would be worth it.

§🐝

"DON'T LOOK AT ME LIKE THAT." BONNIE THREW HER brother the stink eye and returned her attention to the baseball launcher. The final ball sailed through the air, and Bonnie had no problem hitting it with the wooden baseball bat in her hands. She loved the resounding crack and vibration the moment the two connected.

She leaned the bat against the fence and faced Wyatt. "Jace is paying me the same, plus the apartment. It's like a huge raise when you look at it that way. Not having to pay rent is a big thing."

"I'm not arguing with you." Wyatt picked up a bat but didn't move to get into position. "I just want to make sure you've thought everything through. Once you're out there and moved into the apartment, it'll be a lot harder to quit and walk away if you need to."

Bonnie could tell by the look on Wyatt's face that there was something else he wanted to say. She wrinkled her nose at him. "Spill."

"Have you talked to Lew about this? From what you've told me, I can't imagine he'll be happy about you moving out there."

"Not yet." She'd wanted to get Wyatt's impression first, but guilt stabbed at her conscience. "And you're right, he won't be happy. But I love my job, and this will save me a ton of driving and money. Shouldn't Lew be supportive of that?"

"Theoretically, yes, he should." Wyatt paused. "Why are the two of you still together?"

Bonnie wanted to be offended by the question. Instead,

she thought about Lew and their relationship—or the lack of one lately—and shrugged. "I'm trying to be patient. Maybe we just need some time. All I know is that I'm not getting any younger, and it's not like I have a lot of prospects." She sounded pathetic.

Wyatt gave her a sharp look. "It's not like you're an old spinster, Bon. Come on." He lifted his bat and gave an exaggerated swing. "Look, I'm not trying to judge. If you think Lew could be the one, then far be it from me to discourage you from waiting things out. But if he's not…" He shrugged and stepped up to bat.

Before he could get the ball machine started, Bonnie raised her voice. "If he's not, what? I should break up with him?"

Wyatt lowered the bat again. "I know better than to tell you what to do. All I'm saying is that, if it's not Lew, you're not going to meet the right guy as long as it looks like you're already taken." With that, he hit an incoming ball, the sound punctuating what he'd just told her.

Bonnie had never thought about it that way. Wyatt was right, of course. But admitting that and doing something about it was a whole different thing. She'd always imagined getting married and having a family of her own. You know, a normal family, not like the kind she grew up in. The last few years, though, it'd begun to seem more like a dream than an attainable goal. Maybe going out with Lew had given her the illusion that things could work out between them.

She released a heavy sigh. She was only up to one big life decision at a time, and right now, figuring out what to do with her job had to happen first. She'd deal with Lew after that.

Chapter Five

✦❧✦

"There's no going back now." Bonnie's eyes roamed over her new apartment. She'd opted to use the furnishings already there and rented a small storage building to house the few pieces of furniture she owned that were worth keeping. Since she no longer had to pay rent, the storage unit was a no-brainer. Wyatt had helped her move everything a couple of days ago.

Now it was Saturday, she was pretty much moved into her new place, and she was alone. She'd hoped Wyatt and Chrissy might stay and have dinner with her, but Chrissy hadn't been feeling well all day. As soon as Wyatt moved the last box upstairs, he'd left to go help his wife. Bonnie could hardly blame either of them.

Okay, she wasn't completely alone.

She smiled at her guinea pig, Oreo, who remained oblivious of her new surroundings. Of course, her change was minimal since her large cage moved along with her. Lucky guinea pig.

Oreo stuck her black and white head out from the house she was resting in. Bonnie was glad it'd been easy for one of them. She walked to the window in the living room that looked out over the property behind the main house. Was it weird to feel completely at home already? She let one shoulder rest against the frame of the window.

She'd tried to talk to Lew in person over the last week and a half, but his schedule had not allowed for time. Or, as Bonnie suspected, he was avoiding her. Either way, it meant she was forced to let him know about her job change over the phone.

He'd said little, but his voice had been cool. He assured her he'd call her this coming week and they'd get together for dinner, then excused himself and hung up.

Contemplating a change of residence had been way easier than examining her relationship with Lew. Nothing like feeling trapped. Maybe Wyatt was right, and she should break it off. It wasn't like they saw each other much anymore anyway. And Lew had never been supportive of her choice to work as a nanny. He hadn't even offered to help her with the move, not that she'd expected him to.

Jace, on the other hand, had been thorough. Even though he hadn't helped her move, he'd made sure she had all of the keys she needed on Friday, including one for the garage, another for her place, and yet one more for the main house.

Bonnie had to add an additional keyring just to hold them all. She wondered how many times she'd fumble with them before she figured out which one belonged where.

She went to one of the windows in the living area and looked out toward the house. She hadn't seen any sign of Jace or Gunner all day. She had, however, received an invitation from Jace to join them for dinner in an hour. To say Bonnie was nervous was an understatement.

If she were a betting person, she'd guess it was Noel's influence that led to Jace asking her to come over. This was a major blur of lines, something she doubted Jace would have decided on himself.

Noel may be just as curious about Bonnie as she was about her boss's sister.

She pushed away from the window. There was plenty to do to keep herself busy between now and then. She finished putting a few things away before getting a shower and then blow-drying her hair.

By then, it was time to go. Bonnie grabbed her bag and headed out of the door.

It was a short walk along the path to the main house, but it was long enough to assess her doubts about this dinner. She was looking forward to finally meeting Noel. But if they didn't get along, dinner would be awkward, much less living on the property in general.

Bonnie pressed the doorbell, the resulting trill of chimes filtering through the door.

Footsteps followed soon after, and the door opened. A woman smiled brightly at her and ushered her in.

There was no denying this was Jace's sister. They both had the same color hair and eyes. Noel's hair, however, hung nearly to her waist, and her features were much more delicate.

"You must be Bonnie! I'm Noel, it's wonderful to meet you. Come on in. Once we told Gunner you were coming, he got so excited."

As if on cue, the little boy ran into the room and nearly threw himself at Bonnie's legs. She loved that, even though she'd cared for the boy all week, he was still pleased to see her.

Bonnie crouched down to give Gunner a hug. "Hey, buddy! I get to eat dinner with you tonight. Is that going to be fun?"

Gunner nodded emphatically, grabbed her hand, and started tugging her toward the kitchen.

Bonnie laughed as she struggled to stand before he pulled

47

her off balance. "Okay, I'm coming." She glanced at Noel. "He never runs out of energy, does he?"

Noel grinned and ruffled her nephew's hair. "Never."

Gunner continued to pull Bonnie toward the kitchen. Was that where Jace was? She had a hard time picturing him in the kitchen cooking anything. Of course, he had to fix meals for himself and Gunner during the weekends, but it wasn't something she'd ever witnessed.

Suddenly, an image of him in an apron formed in Bonnie's mind, and she had to stifle a giggle.

It didn't matter who was cooking the meal, it smelled delicious.

Growing up, her parents always had fancy food at the evening meal. To the point where she often wished she could simply have a bowl of macaroni and cheese or a hot dog like many of her friends.

Jace always stocked what she considered normal food for her to use to fix lunches for Gunner. And the dinners she often made for him were just as easy. But she'd never fixed a meal for Jace.

Did he eat as extravagantly as her parents did?

They entered the kitchen to find him standing at the stove stirring something in a pan. He offered her a smile. "Good evening."

"Good evening," she replied. At least he wasn't in an apron. She couldn't have survived that experience without laughing. "Thank you for the invitation." What she wasn't prepared for, though, was the sight of Jace in something besides his normal work suits. This evening, he wore jeans along with a long-sleeved button-up shirt. Boots completed the ensemble.

She'd always thought he was handsome in the suits he wore, but this? Yeah, if he was going to wear something like this every day, then working on the ranch was going to look real good on him.

Gunner tugged on her hand. "Eat tows! Bon eat tows too?"

Bonnie looked at Jace in question.

He laughed. "Tacos. We're having tacos, and Gunner is quite excited."

Tacos. Okay, that sounded amazing. And like a normal thing to eat. She was surprised by how relieved she was by that.

Apparently, her thoughts had shown on her face. Jace raised an eyebrow at her. "You were expecting something else?"

How did she explain her thoughts without sounding rude? "Growing up, whenever we had company over for a meal, my parents pulled out all the frills. Food was weird and the evening stuffy. It's nice that you all eat normally."

"I'm glad to hear that you do as well." Jace smiled at her again, his eyes a combination of amusement and something else she couldn't quite put her finger on. "You met my sister, Noel?"

"Yes, I did." Bonnie turned to find Noel watching them with interest. "Did you get settled in this week? It takes much longer to unpack than anything else. At least in my experience."

"Most definitely. It helps not having to bring furniture in. It's a bit of a drive since I work on the other side of Clearwater, but I don't mind. Sometimes that drive is the favorite part of my day." Noel pulled her hair around with one hand and let it go again. "How about you?"

"Honestly? It was the easiest move I've ever made since the apartment was already furnished. Your grandparents had beautiful taste."

"I always thought so, too, thank you." Noel smiled, but

there was a hint of sadness in it. "Being here reminds me of them."

"Lots of mixed emotions, I'm sure." Bonnie could certainly understand that. While she never knew her dad's parents, she recalled the grief when her maternal grandfather passed some years ago. She was glad she still had her Gran here with them.

Gunner plopped himself down on the floor near one of the cabinets and pulled several small bowls and a spoon out of it.

"Is there anything I can do to help?"

Jace hesitated. "How are you at cutting tomatoes?"

"I can hold my own." Bonnie smiled when Jace handed her a knife, cutting board, and then motioned to the fridge.

"Tomatoes are in the bottom drawer."

By the time Bonnie retrieved the tomatoes, Gunner had abandoned the pots and pans and was running into the other room. Bonnie's instinct was to follow him since she normally had to keep a close eye on the little boy to make sure he didn't get into any trouble.

Noel set down the cheese she was grating. "I've got him."

With that, Jace and Bonnie were alone in the kitchen.

Bonnie cleared her throat and got to work slicing tomatoes. That didn't take long. Since Noel hadn't returned, she moved to finish grating the cheese.

They worked in silence until Jace finally spoke near the stove. "What was your least favorite fancy meal that your parents served?"

There were a number of meals Bonnie couldn't stand to this day. But one in particular stood out. "Sushi. My mom loves it, and we had it once a week." She made a face and shuddered, still remembering the first time she'd tasted it. "Mom always figured if she could stomach something, the rest of us could, too. Alternative meals were never an option."

Jace nodded, his face sympathetic. "I'm not a sushi fan,

either. I'm not big on seafood of any kind, to be honest." He put the lid on the pan containing the taco meat and turned the heat on low. "Noel and I liked most of what we ate as kids. But we had a nanny who was amazing and understood what kids actually preferred to eat." He paused. "I appreciate that you are the same with Gunner."

She dipped her chin in acknowledgment of his compliment. "My siblings and I didn't have a dedicated nanny, but there were several women that came into our lives at different times. They were kind and fun. I guess that's why I wanted to be a nanny myself."

"How many brothers and sisters do you have?" The question came from Noel as she reentered the kitchen. Gunner followed her with a push toy that made popping sounds as he moved it across the floor.

"I have two older sisters and one brother. Wyatt and I are the closest, though. I spend a lot of time with him and his wife, Chrissy." Bonnie smiled as she thought about them. "They are expecting a baby early next year. This will be my first niece or nephew that I'll have the chance to be involved with. I'm looking forward to it."

"That's great!" Noel smiled. "Being an aunt is the best."

Bonnie nodded. She had other nieces and nephews but only saw them once or twice a year during family gatherings. She looked forward to being a part of this new baby's life on a regular basis.

"It looks like we're about ready to eat," Jace announced.

They all helped take food to the square table that was just big enough for the four of them. Bonnie ended up sitting with Jace to her right and Noel to her left. She waved to Gunner across from her.

"Let's pray." As soon as the words left Jace's mouth, he hesitated.

Bonnie watched as Gunner reached for his dad's hand and then his aunt's. Noel held a hand out to Bonnie, who took it.

But it was the sensation of Jace's strong hand clasping hers that had Bonnie struggling to focus on his words as he blessed their meal.

As soon as he finished, everyone said, "Amen."

Jace released her hand and cleared his throat.

Bonnie tried to ignore the way her own still tingled even though he was no longer touching it. When Jace handed her a platter, she accepted it, thankful for the distraction.

JACE OBJECTED THE FIRST TIME NOEL INSISTED THEY INVITE Bonnie for dinner. He didn't want to blur the line between work and personal life. But the more Noel explained why she thought they should, the less he could argue.

He wanted Bonnie to see the ranch as home and to know that if she needed anything, all she had to do was call or come by. If it were Noel working in a similar situation, he would be happy knowing that she was well taken care of.

He hadn't thought about their custom of holding hands while praying, though. They'd never done it at home growing up, but it was always something they did here at the ranch with their grandparents.

It'd been as natural as breathing. Until Bonnie's hand was nestled in his as though it belonged there. He hadn't antici-pated the way his heart raced in response or the keen disap-pointment when she withdrew it again after the prayer.

Thankfully, everyone focused on filling their plates. Conversation stayed at a minimum, allowing Jace's pulse to return to normal as he focused on something else.

Satisfied that Gunner had everything he needed, Jace

filled three taco shells with the seasoned meat. His stomach growled in anticipation.

Partway through the meal, Noel patted her stomach. "I could eat tacos any day of the week. You know, maybe this could be a thing? We have tacos and eat together every Saturday night?" She looked from Bonnie to Jace expectantly.

Jace had no idea what to say. The fact that he immediately looked forward to seeing Bonnie again at dinner next week told him it was a terrible idea.

Thankfully, Bonnie spoke up. "I'm not sure I can promise that. I try to help out at my brother's stables most Saturdays. And the guy I'm seeing usually likes to set up dates on Friday or Saturday nights."

Jace immediately disliked the guy. He wanted to know more about their relationship, but Jace said nothing.

Noel took it all in stride. "Then you can join us on the Saturdays you're here." As though that settled everything, she changed the subject. "Your brother owns stables? Does that mean you ride?"

Bonnie nodded. "Wyatt and I have always enjoyed horseback riding. I don't get to ride nearly as often as I'd like, though." She wiped her hands off on a napkin and laid it across her plate. "He owns and runs Joyful Hope Stables. I like to help with some of the hippotherapy sessions."

Jace tried to wrap his mind around everything he was learning about Bonnie. She was seeing a guy she didn't call her boyfriend, she rode horses, and she volunteered to help in therapy sessions.

He'd known none of this about Bonnie because he'd never asked her personal questions. Now he was second-guessing himself. There was being professional, and then there was indifference.

He and Noel had grown up with parents who were largely

uninterested in everything related to their children, and a number of hired caregivers who were as well.

He'd managed to find someone amazing who truly cared about his son. But was he treating her the way he'd loathed being treated himself growing up?

The thought bothered him a great deal. He'd always sworn he'd be nothing like his parents. But in keeping up such a definite wall between himself and Bonnie, had he inadvertently become someone he never wanted to be?

Gunner finished eating and proudly brandished his messy hands. The adults all chuckled.

Jace tried his best to clean his son's hands, but the paper towels were no match.

Noel stood. "I'll go give him a bath."

Bonnie stood as well. "I had better head out myself."

Jace followed suit and wished the evening didn't have to end. He'd learned a lot about Bonnie, and that information was addicting. What else didn't he know about her?

Noel extracted Gunner from his highchair. "It was nice to meet you, Bonnie. I'm looking forward to getting to know you better. I'm glad you joined us for dinner." Gunner got some shredded cheese in her hair. Noel's nose wrinkled. "Looks like he's not the only one who is going to need a bath."

Bonnie laughed. "It was great to meet you, too. Thank you both for the invitation." She tickled Gunner on the tummy. "And I will see you on Monday, little guy. Bye, bye!" She waved to him.

Gunner waved back, his palm facing him and his fingers moving up and down.

Jace loved the way he waved and knew that it wouldn't last long before he realized how to do it correctly.

He watched as Noel carried Gunner out of the dining room.

"It's great that your sister helps with Gunner so much."

Jace nodded. "It is a blessing, that's for sure." His own parents had never been willing to help. Their unkind words spoken after Gunner was born came to mind, and he did everything he could to shove them back into the closet of his mind where they belonged.

They looked at each other for several moments. Bonnie shifted her weight from one foot to the other. "I can help you clean up."

"Oh, don't worry about it. I'll put everything in the dishwasher. It won't take long." Their time spent in the kitchen cooking together was about as domestic as they needed to get for one night. "Do you have everything you need at the apartment? If anything's missing, please let me know."

"Are you kidding? The place is great. I actually feel guilty I'm not paying any rent at all." She gave him a tentative smile. "Thank you again."

"No problem." He watched as she retrieved her bag and got ready to leave.

They reached the door, and she lifted a hand in farewell. "Have a good night, Jace."

"You, too."

Jace closed the door behind her before going upstairs and standing near the alcove. He watched until she appeared on the path and entered the garage. Only then did he go into the kitchen and get to work.

He was nearly finished when Noel returned with a squeaky-clean Gunner in tow.

"How does one toddler get this much food in his hair?"

Jace laughed. "I wish I knew the answer to that."

Gunner began to play with magnets on the fridge.

Noel took a towel from Jace and dried the kitchen counter. "So. Bonnie sure is nice."

"Yep."

His sister abandoned the towel and turned to face him, her hands on her hips. "You've definitely got a keeper. Gunner obviously adores her, that's clear."

"Yep." Noel obviously had more to say, and Jace chose to wait her out. It didn't take long.

"And you've never once thought about dating her?" Noel's voice was quiet. She was the only other person who knew the details of his relationship with Samantha and how things had gotten rocky before Gunner was born.

"Nope." Okay, that was a lie. But thinking about it and acting on it were two entirely different things.

"Samantha would want you to move on, Jace."

The mention of his wife's name ignited a pang of sadness. He knew Noel was right. Samantha would want him to live his life and be happy. But that didn't mean getting married again was in the cards for him. It was easier to not argue with Noel, though. "Bonnie's boyfriend might object." He flashed Noel his best, "So there," expression.

"Hmmm." With that, Noel raised an eyebrow, clearly not convinced.

"She's just Gunner's nanny, Noel." The tone in his voice would normally make the men who used to work under him snap to attention. Too bad it didn't work as well on his sister.

Chapter Six

❧

J ace's boots created a satisfying thud on the porch steps as he descended. It was six o'clock in the morning. He remembered well how Grandpa was always awake early, and he'd spoken with the ranch foreman, Cabe Yates, about when they started work.

There were many times Jace would scramble from his bed as a kid, throw on cowboy boots that were way too big, and go running off after Grandpa to help with the ranch chores. Noel would stay behind with Grandma and help with things around the house until Grandma passed away. By then, Noel insisted on keeping up the house herself for the first half of the day before joining them at lunch.

Grief tightened around his heart while his resolve to keep this ranch running grew stronger. But to do that, he had to learn the ins and outs of what it took to maintain it.

Cabe started working for Grandpa when he was only eighteen and had stayed on for nearly thirty years. There was no one better to teach Jace about the ranch.

Jace got settled in his F-150 King Ranch pickup. He drove past the garage and wondered whether Bonnie was awake yet, or if she was still asleep. She always arrived at work ready to face the day. Was she an early riser as well?

Not that it was any of his business.

He drove along the dirt road that led through the trees that acted as a visual barrier between the house and the large barn beyond.

It was there that Cabe had his own quarters in the apartment above. Cabe, a self-proclaimed bachelor, had been working for Grandpa for nearly as long as Jace could remember.

The older gentleman waited for Jace, his back pressed against the barn wall. As soon as Jace stepped out of the truck, Cabe walked forward, a hand outstretched. "Good to see you again, Jace."

"You, too." Jace had been out several times in the last week to talk to Cabe and get an idea of what all he needed to get acquainted with there on the ranch. Today, he'd be jumping in and taking over for Grandpa.

They were big shoes to fill.

As though Cabe could read his mind, he gave a definitive nod. "Your grandfather would be real proud of you."

"I appreciate that. I just hope I can get everything figured out. Working here over the summer as a kid doesn't exactly qualify me as a rancher."

The idea that he might fail Grandpa in any way bothered him more than he cared to admit.

Cabe shot him a sympathetic look. "Your grandfather believed in you. Always did say you were a natural. I've worked with him for nearly thirty years and not once did he speak of you with anything but pride." He tipped his head toward the pistol at Jace's hip. "That your grandfather's piece?"

"It is." Jace placed a hand on the wooden hilt. Grandpa carried it with him everywhere on the ranch. It's what Jace learned to shoot with, too. Wearing it himself made Jace feel closer to Grandpa somehow.

He also knew how important it was to be armed while working the ranch.

Cabe—always the type to get right to the job at hand—seemed ready to set the reminiscing aside. "First, I'll introduce you to the guys your grandpa hired to help around here. They are unloading feed around back."

As they walked around the barn, Jace saw two men in their late twenties working together to unload bags of feed and stack them in the barn. They both immediately stopped what they were doing and stepped forward.

Cabe cleared his throat. "This is Jace Echolls, Jethro's grandson. Jace, this here is Brady," the men shook hands, "and this is Elvin."

Jace shook the second man's hand as well. "Good to meet you. Had you worked for my grandfather long?"

Brady tipped his head in respect. "Five years next month, sir. He was a good man. I'm sorry for your loss."

"I appreciate that." Jace turned his attention to Elvin.

"Been working here for over eight years," the man said. He spat chewing tobacco into the dirt.

Jace didn't react, although just the smell of chewing tobacco had always been a deterrent for him. "I have no doubt the two of you have been instrumental in helping Grandpa run this place. I appreciate that."

Cabe nodded with satisfaction. "As you all know, Jace and his sister, Noel, are now living on the ranch and will be running it."

"If you have any questions or concerns, please let me know," Jace said.

Brady gave them a friendly wave while Elvin simply nodded. The men returned to their work.

Cabe motioned Jace forward. "Let's go. By the time I'm

done with you today, you'll know exactly what's going on with the ranch."

The guy wasn't kidding, either. Jace's head swam with specifics about the ranch and where it was financially. He had pages in a notepad full of information about the sheep and what Grandpa had planned for the rest of the year. Jace didn't realize it was possible to be simultaneously confused and enlightened .

One thing he knew for sure, though, was that he intended to learn the ins and outs of this ranch no matter how long it took. He told Cabe as much. "The only way I'm going to learn is through experience. If there's a problem with the sheep or anything I should be aware of, call me night or day."

There was a hint of pride in Cabe's eyes. "I'll do it. I'm looking forward to seeing that son of yours again. He's quite the spitfire."

"That he is. We'd love if you'd join us for dinner Sunday night."

"I'll be there. One of these days, we'll have to get you and Noel out here on a horse again. Maybe teach Gunner to ride."

Jace nodded thoughtfully. He couldn't imagine trying to get his young son on a horse anytime soon. He was way too active for that. But maybe Gunner would sit with Jace on the saddle for a while.

Otherwise, Bonnie could watch him. Or maybe she could come with them…

That the thought had even crossed his mind had Jace scrambling to block it. He looked over to find Cabe watching him curiously. Cabe looked as though he were about to say something when Jace's phone rang.

Jace was happy for the distraction until he saw Bonnie's name on the caller ID. He could count on one hand the number of times she'd called him, and every time it was because something was going on with Gunner.

He answered the call. "This is Jace. Everything okay?"

"Hey, I'm sorry to bother you." Her voice sounded breathless which only kicked his worry up a notch. "I took Gunner outside for a while. We ran into a rattlesnake. Gunner's fine--we both are--but the snake is right up here by the house…"

The last thing Jace wanted to worry about was a rattlesnake where his son was playing. "Keep your distance, but try to keep track of it. I'll be there as soon as I can." He ended the call and turned to Cabe. "Bonnie ran into a rattlesnake at the house. I'm going to go take care of it and I'll be back."

Cabe nodded his agreement. "I've killed several in the last couple of weeks. That the nanny?"

"Yep."

"You might consider teaching her how to shoot if she doesn't know how to already."

Jace imagined doing just that, his hands on hers as he taught her how to properly hold a gun. If the way his pulse jumped was any indication, it was a situation he should probably avoid like the plague.

BONNIE STOOD IN THE FRONT YARD, POWERLESS TO DO anything about the snake. A frustrated Gunner wailed in her arms as she watched the reptile from a safe distance.

She hadn't been around them much, but she knew enough to guess that it was probably cold from the night before and was soaking up warmth from the sun's rays. Hopefully, it would stay put until Jace got there.

If the snake slithered away, Bonnie wouldn't be able to

come outside in the near future without expecting to see it again. At least she'd spotted it before Gunner had gone anywhere close to it. She shuddered again when she thought about what might have happened.

She just wished she hadn't had to call Jace at all.

Despite the guilt of knowing she'd interrupted his work-day, relief flooded her system when she saw his blue truck come around the corner and park nearby.

He got out and jogged over, concern on his face. "Both of you are okay?"

Gunner reached for him, but Jace only patted him on the back.

Bonnie nodded. "Yes, I saw it long before Gunner got anywhere near it."

"Thank God." He withdrew his gun and held it close, barrel toward the ground. "Where is it?"

She pointed to where the snake was stretched out.

"Take Gunner inside, please, that way the shot doesn't hurt his ears. I'll come in when I'm done."

Bonnie shifted Gunner in her arms and headed for the house. They weren't inside long before the sound of a gunshot told her the snake was gone.

Gunner obliviously kicked a ball around the kitchen floor.

True to his word, Jace walked in not long later. "All taken care of. Cabe, the guy who has been running the ranch since Grandpa passed, said he's killed several in the last couple of weeks. I guess keep an eye out."

Bonnie nodded. "I thought about getting a shovel and killing it that way, but I didn't want to risk setting Gunner down to do it." And the idea of getting close enough to kill it with a shovel didn't sit well with her. But she would've done it if she had to. "Again, I'm sorry to have interrupted you at work."

He shot her a firm look. "If you, or Gunner, ever need

something, it's not an interruption." The tone of his voice told her he was being serious. "It's not like before where I'd have to walk out of conference calls or leave the office. I'm only a few minutes away here. It's never any trouble."

He watched her with an intensity that captured her gaze and made it hard to look away.

Gunner drove his car across the floor and crashed it into Jace's boot, snagging the attention of both adults.

Jace reached down and ruffled his son's hair. "Whoa, big guy." He knelt down. "I've got to get back to work. Behave yourself, okay?" He pulled the little boy into his arms for a brief hug before Gunner was off and running again.

Bonnie pushed some hair behind her ear and cleared her throat. "Thanks for taking care of the snake, Jace."

He nodded once before walking back toward the front door. Bonnie followed. He'd just opened it to leave when he turned again and lightly touched her arm.

"Thank you for keeping Gunner safe."

With that, he pivoted and left, but not before his fingers had effectively set her skin on fire. She placed a cool hand over it and forced herself to take a calming breath. She watched as her boss—a businessman turned rancher—got back in his truck and drove away.

Her phone pinged just then, and she looked to find a message from Lew. "Dinner Saturday at five?"

Saved by the boyfriend—the man she ought to be focused on. It was hard to ignore the fact that a simple touch from Jace had more effect on her than Lew ever had.

Chapter Seven

The moment Bonnie opened the door and saw Lew's face, she knew he wasn't happy. It wasn't so much the way the corners of his mouth were angled down as the critical look in his eyes.

She'd offered to meet him in Clearwater, but Lew insisted on picking her up. She suspected he wanted to see where she was living now. She couldn't blame him. But he clearly found it lacking.

Bonnie tamped down her annoyance and tried to put a normal smile on her face. "Hey, I'm glad you found it. Isn't it pretty out here?"

"It took even longer to get here than I thought. We're going to be late for our reservation."

"I was hoping to give you a tour of my apartment..." The moment the words left her lips, it was clear Lew had no interest. "Let me grab my bag, and I'll be ready to go."

Once she was, Lew escorted her to his Mercedes where she slid into the passenger seat. Normally, she would've pointed out some things—like the sheep she could see in a nearby pasture. Instead, she clasped her hands in her lap and dug a thumbnail into the side of one of her fingers.

All the way back to Clearwater, Lew spoke of nothing but his work and how long it was taking for them to get to town again. Not once did he ask if she was settled into her new place.

Considering he hadn't bothered to talk to her since the night she'd worked late, his reactions were entirely too petty.

They'd been growing apart for a while, but Bonnie hadn't realized just how self-centered he was until she'd made the decision to move to the ranch without his approval. Ever since then, he'd made it clear he was unhappy and seemed completely uninterested in anything she had to say about the subject.

Once they'd parked, Lew opened her door and then captured her hand in his. The first thing that entered Bonnie's mind was the way a touch from Jace had sent tingles zipping up and down her skin. Here with Lew? There was none of that.

Was it her? Surely it was. The thought was depressing.

She bit back a sigh. *God, I wish I knew what was going on here. For a while there, I thought Lew might be the one. Maybe I was just being hopeful.* Or she was completely clueless.

After all, Mom often insisted it didn't bode well that she was in her thirties and still hadn't gotten married. Bonnie didn't agree, but it was nearly impossible to keep those criticizing words from invading her thoughts.

Mom always made sure to point out all of Bonnie's flaws and make up some more. It'd frustrated Bonnie to no end. It's a good thing she had a healthy dose of self-confidence. But what if her mom was right about at least some of it?

One thing was certain: She had to stop tying herself to a relationship that wasn't meant to be.

Am I supposed to break up with Lew? Some kind of sign would be great, God.

Lew remained silent as they were shown to their table. It wasn't until after they placed their order that he finally focused all of his attention on her.

"You should move back to town."

Bonnie blinked at him. "I can't do that. It'd mean losing my job. Finding somewhere else to live." The consequences of such a decision made her light-headed. Besides, she'd gone through this entire thought process before accepting the change in her job location, and she was more certain now than ever that she'd made the right choice.

"You can come work for my company. I could get you a job as a receptionist tomorrow." He watched her closely, his lips pressed together.

Work as a receptionist? There was nothing wrong with the job, but she loved her position as a nanny and couldn't imagine trading her time with Gunner for a desk. She shook her head.

"You could move in with me," Lew continued. "Then you wouldn't need an apartment at all. At least we'd see more of each other."

Bonnie's stomach ached as tears came to her eyes. They'd had this discussion more than once. She'd made it clear that she wasn't comfortable moving in with a guy unless they were married. He'd said he understood. Now she wondered just how true that was.

The waiter brought a welcome distraction as food was placed before them. To Bonnie, nothing about the manicotti steaming on her plate looked or smelled good.

In contrast, Lew dug right into his meatless lasagna.

Their meal was consumed in near-silence. Any attempts Bonnie made to direct their conversation to something safer was met with one-word replies.

A third of the way through her manicotti, she finally gave up and placed her napkin on top of her plate.

Lew had no problem finishing his meal. It was only after he'd set his fork down that he leveled his gaze on her. "Move back into Clearwater, Bonnie. Move in with me."

In that moment, even though Bonnie had no idea what her future held, she knew that Lew wasn't going to be in it. When she'd asked God for a sign, she hadn't anticipated a blasted neon one hitting her right in the forehead.

"This isn't working, Lew. *We're* not working."

He lifted a single brow as he stared at her. "You can't be serious."

"I'm not quitting my job. And we've had this discussion before: I'm not moving in with you. I love being a nanny. I can't imagine not working with children." She shook her head. "The Echolls ranch is where I belong." Her voice softened. "Things haven't been right between us for a while. I think you know that as well as I do."

There was no missing the intense disapproval on Lew's face. He tossed his napkin onto the table and stood. He withdrew money from his wallet and placed it on the table. "Take care of yourself, Bonnie."

"Wait, Lew. What about taking me back to my apartment?"

One side of his mouth rose an iota. "Why don't you call Jace Echolls for a ride?" With that, he turned on his heel and left the dining area.

Bonnie sat and stared at her water glass. The flowers on the other side of the liquid appeared distorted. Changed.

Just like her life.

Tears burned behind her eyelids, but they weren't tears of sadness or even embarrassment. She didn't regret breaking up with Lew. Anger and annoyance were the cause of her tears, and much of it was directed at herself for letting things with Lew last this long.

Her chest tightened, and her throat ached. She'd wasted months with him.

Numbly, she glanced at her watch. Wyatt was still teaching a class at the stables and wouldn't be free for another hour. Bonnie didn't want to call Chrissy since she might be sleeping. She'd take a walk. Clear her head. Then call her brother to give her a ride back to the ranch.

The only solace right now was knowing that Wyatt would threaten to hunt Lew down for leaving Bonnie stranded like this.

She might very well let him.

"THANKS FOR THE HELP REPAIRING THE BARN ROOF." CABE pulled to a stop in front of the main house and held a hand out to Jace. "I think we got that hole patched in record time."

Jace shook the older man's hand. "Not a problem." When Cabe had mentioned water leaked through the roof during the last rainstorm, Jace had volunteered to lend a hand. Cabe had picked him up at the house first thing Saturday morning. Jace promised Noel he'd be back before lunch, and here it wasn't even eleven yet.

A fancy black car approached and parked in front of the house. A man got out wearing a suit, complete with tie, and a briefcase in his right hand.

Jace didn't recognize him. "Let me see what this guy is up to." He got out of Cabe's truck and approached their visitor. "Is there something I can help you with?"

The man handed Jace a business card. "Milton Hays. I work for Hays and Patterson Real Estate. I wondered if you had a few moments."

Movement at the front door caught Jace's eye and he saw Noel watching them with a quizzical look on her face. Jace turned his attention back to Mr. Hays. "I only have a moment. What is this about?"

"I've got a client who would very much like to buy this property. Perhaps we could go inside and talk some numbers?" The man turned toward the house, the sun shining off his slightly greasy hair.

"I'm just going to stop you right there. We're not interested in selling this place, and I sure would hate to waste your time."

"I've got a purchase price you might not be able to refuse." Mr. Hays pulled his briefcase up and started to open it.

Jace shook his head. "I'm not selling this place for any price. Please relay that to your client. I hope you have a wonderful Saturday afternoon, sir." With that, Jace escorted the guy back to his car accompanied with some sputtering and objections that Jace chose to ignore.

Mr. Hays's face was red as he got into his car and closed the door behind him.

Jace stood there, his hands to his sides, until the car disappeared from sight. Only then did he go back to Cabe's truck. "Sorry about that. Hopefully he'll let his client know we're not selling, and that'll be the end of it."

Cabe hitched a thumb in the direction of the realtor's car. "You weren't even curious about the offer?" He chuckled dryly.

"Nope." He waved to Noel in the doorway. "Thanks again for the ride, Cabe. Have a good rest of your Saturday."

"You, too."

Jace stepped into the house to find Noel waiting for him, clearly curious about the conversation. He told her about the realtor and what all was said. Only then did he notice she was squinting a little. "You getting one of your headaches?"

Noel nodded and flinched. "I've been fighting it with everything I can think of, but it's not helping much."

Noel got bad headaches frequently, but this looked like the beginning of a migraine. He glanced at Gunner who was noisily playing in the living room. "Tell you what. I haven't had lunch yet. How about I take Gunner into Clearwater. We'll get something to eat, play at the park, go to the mall, and I'll bring back dinner later?"

Noel smiled gratefully. "Have I mentioned you're the best big brother ever?"

He shrugged. "I have an occasional stroke of brilliance."

She laughed then, but the crinkles in the corners of her eyes revealed her discomfort. "Thanks, Jace."

JACE WHISTLED ALONG WITH THE RADIO STATION AS HE DROVE his truck through Clearwater. It'd been a busy afternoon with Gunner. By the time Jace went to the supply store, the park, and the mall, his young son was completely worn out. They hadn't been in the truck more than five minutes and the little guy was passed out cold in his car seat.

Now Jace planned to go through a drive-through and get one of Noel's favorite meals to take back to the ranch.

Jace glanced at his son in the rearview mirror and smiled. He'd already seen more of Gunner since they moved to the ranch than he had the previous two months combined. Not only that, but Jace experienced less stress than he had in longer than he could remember. Normally, he was already going through the list of meetings coming up in the next week. Today? He'd simply enjoyed spending time with his son.

The move he'd agonized over was undoubtedly one of the best decisions he'd ever made.

His mind flitted to Bonnie. He hoped she was happy with her apartment and the new job arrangement. What was she doing right now? Noel had invited Bonnie to join them for dinner, but Bonnie said she had plans. And yes, he'd noticed that her car was still in front of the garage when he left.

He could only assume her boyfriend had come to pick her up.

Jace's earlier good mood faded. It was none of his business what Bonnie was doing on her day off. Whether she was shopping, going out with her boyfriend, or robbing a bank. Okay, maybe that last one would affect him somewhat. He chuckled to himself.

He drove through a crowded area in downtown Clearwater. A woman walking along the sidewalk ahead caught his eye. It couldn't be.

She turned to cut across a parking lot. The moment she did, it was as though the subject of his thoughts materialized right before his eyes.

Acting on instinct, he turned into the parking lot and rolled his window down as he pulled up beside her.

She glanced at him and her eyes widened. He barely saw a stray tear on her cheek before she brushed it away and forced a smile. "Hey, you're about the last person I expected to run into."

"Are you okay?"

"Sure. Just taking a walk." The shaky undertone of her voice contradicted her words.

Jace glanced around. "Where are you heading?" He didn't want to push her, but he sure wasn't going to leave her out here when she was clearly upset, either. Where was her boyfriend, and why wasn't he escorting Bonnie?

Bonnie took in her surroundings as though she hadn't been paying attention to where she was going. Finally, she shrugged. "My brother gets off work in about thirty minutes.

Truthfully, I'm just killing time. I was going to call and ask him for a ride home." She bit her lower lip then.

As long as Jace had known Bonnie, she was the picture of composure.

Until now.

The vulnerability in her eyes had his heart turning over in his chest.

"I was headed back to the ranch. Why don't you just ride with us?"

Bonnie stood on her tiptoes to look through the window into the back seat where Gunner was still sleeping. "He always looks so cute and innocent when he falls asleep like that."

"Yeah, he does." And once the boy was asleep, little woke him up. "Come on, hop in."

Bonnie hesitated several moments before walking around the front of the truck and climbing into the passenger seat.

The radio was still on, and since Bonnie didn't seem to be in the mood to talk, he left it playing to fill the void.

Once back on the ranch, he drove past the house to the garage, her vehicle still parked out front.

Jace put the truck in park and turned to look at Bonnie just in time to notice her chin quiver. She turned her head toward the window and some of her hair fell down to hide her face. "Thanks for the ride."

Before she got out of the car, Jace reached for her arm to stop her. "What happened, Bonnie?" She said nothing, and he pushed a little harder. "Did he hurt you?"

Bonnie immediately shook her head. "No. Nothing like that." She shrugged. "He hated that I kept this job and moved out here. He wanted me to quit and move in with him." Her voice caught. She turned and looked at Gunner, her eyes full of emotion. "He knows I love my job, and that moving in with him was never an option. I broke up with him tonight."

Jace's instantaneous relief at that news surprised him. He ought to feel guilty about that. Instead, Jace kept his "good riddance" comment to himself. "He left you to find your own way back home, didn't he?" She nodded. It was proof that Lew was certainly no gentleman, and a first-class jerk to boot. "I'm sorry, Bonnie."

"It's for the best. I've managed this long on my own, I'll be just fine." She offered him a shaky smile. "Lew said he loved me. I just wish I'd realized the truth sooner."

Jace swallowed hard. If he knew where to find Lew, he'd hunt him down and give him a piece of his mind.

"I'm no expert on relationships." The one he'd had with Samantha was anything but perfect. "I may not have love figured out, but I can tell you that treating you the way Lew did isn't love. Bonnie, you deserve better."

Jace dropped his hand then, when what he wanted to do was pull her into a hug. The intensity of that need had him grasping for some measure of sanity. Forget crossing a line. Hugging his son's nanny would be akin to erasing it.

"Thanks. For the ride, and your kind words." Bonnie sniffed and lifted her chin a little. "I'll be okay. I'd been praying about it and hoping for a sign. Just didn't expect it to be quite so blatant."

She chuckled a little then. Even though she seemed far from okay, at least some of her humor was returning. Jace offered what he hoped was a comforting smile. "Let us know if you need anything, okay?"

Bonnie gave a small nod. "Thanks again." She motioned to the back seat. "You'd better get him home and wake him up or he'll never sleep tonight."

Jace shook his head. "Yeah, it might be too late for that."

With a final wave, Bonnie got out of his car and disappeared into the garage.

His heart ached as he thought about the pain she was

going through right now. Maybe he didn't know Bonnie as well as he should, but one thing was certain: Lew was an idiot to let her go.

❧

BONNIE CLOSED HER APARTMENT DOOR BEHIND HER AND leaned against it with a heavy sigh. This day had not ended the way she ever would have guessed.

Sure, she figured Lew was going to give her a hard time. His lack of communication and disdain for her job before had given her a heads up. But it hadn't been until she'd moved here to the ranch that she'd seen his true colors.

And then there was Jace.

Whether he realized it or not, Jace had been her hero. If only she hadn't spilled the whole story about Lew.

Bonnie groaned and let the back of her head connect solidly with the door behind her.

She hadn't intended to tell him what Lew said about her job, and especially not about him asking her to move in with him.

But Jace had been there, the definition of support, his eyes full of concern. Before she knew it, she'd told him everything. Or at least an abridged version of it.

Jace was right, though. There's no way Lew ever truly loved her. If he did, he would've fought for their relationship. He would've made some effort to understand her.

The sad thing, though, was while she was hurt and angry, there was also an undertone of relief. She'd been worried about Lew being angry ever since she moved out to the ranch. The truth was, she was never in love with him, either.

Her thoughts hovered on Jace. Her employer had been kinder to her tonight than Lew had been in a long time.

What she needed was a hot shower, a good cry, and some

ice cream. Then she had every intention of leaving Lew in the dust where he belonged.

The sound of Oreo wheeking from her cage drew Bonnie over. The guinea pig was on her hind legs, front feet against the bars, as she asked for attention in the only way she knew how. With each wheek, her little ears lifted. The sight made Bonnie smile. "Hey, girl. Thanks for waiting up for me." Bonnie opened the cage and ran a hand over the soft fur. "Let me grab you a treat before I go take a shower."

A few minutes later, Oreo gratefully snagged the piece of carrot from Bonnie's hand and dragged it into her hay house where she munched happily.

Too bad Bonnie's mood couldn't be as easily improved.

By the time she got out of the shower, she felt a little better. The hot water had washed away her tears, and she was content to slip into comfortable clothes and settle down with a pint of ice cream.

Bonnie checked her phone, surprised to find a text from Jace waiting for her.

"Take care of yourself. You are in my prayers."

Tears threatened again, but this time it was because his words were like a balm to her wounded heart.

Suddenly, with Lew out of the picture, Jace's presence became much more prominent. All of her original reasons for why she couldn't fall for her boss were still just as valid as they were before. She'd do well to remember that.

Tomorrow.

For tonight, she'd let Jace play the part of a one-time white knight. Surely there was no harm in that.

Chapter Eight

❧❧❧

Concern coursed through Jace quickly followed by annoyance as he studied the damaged fence.

Cabe took the glove off his right hand and leaned in for a better look. "The cuts are clean. Someone did this on purpose." He touched the smooth edge of a damaged panel with his bare thumb.

Six panels of fencing were on the ground, leaving a space plenty large enough for a vehicle to drive through. Certainly enough room for sheep to escape. Thankfully, most of the flock was in a different pasture.

Cabe shook his head. "We're going to have to get this fixed and soon. I'll take the truck and go into town for panels."

"And I'll make sure all sheep are out of this section and stay close by. I don't want to leave Bonnie and Gunner here by themselves."

"Sounds good." Cabe slipped his glove back on. "I'll let you know when I'm back. Barring anything unexpected, we can have this repaired before nightfall."

With a plan in place, the men went their separate ways.

Jace checked on the rest of the sheep. It didn't look like

any were missing. A blessing considering that, had the fence been cut in a different pasture, things could've been much worse.

But why would someone cut the fencing if they hadn't intended to steal some of the sheep?

He was still contemplating different scenarios when he got back to the house. He noted the door was unlocked like normal and frowned. For the first time since they'd moved to the ranch, he wondered whether that was the best thing to do.

"Bonnie?"

When there was no answer, he headed upstairs. He was halfway there when he heard Gunner's happy squeal and Bonnie's voice drifting toward him. It was only then that he realized how important it was that he needed to know they were safe—both of them.

He found them in Gunner's room building a raceway out of blocks. Bonnie sat on the floor with him, a smile on her face as the boy steered a car haphazardly through the racecourse.

She lifted her eyes and her gaze met Jace's. Her smile fell as she got to her feet. "Is everything okay?"

"Look, Daddy!" Gunner shoved a race car, causing it to crash into the railing of the track and careen out of control.

"Great job, buddy! You've got an awesome racetrack there." He smiled at his son before turning his attention back to Bonnie. "Someone intentionally damaged a large section of fencing. It doesn't look like we lost any sheep, but I don't know why someone would do this otherwise." He paused. "I'd prefer it if you'd lock the doors here when I'm gone. And I recommend you keep your apartment—and the garage door—locked as well."

Bonnie ran her fingers through her hair, her lips pursed. "Well, that's not creepy at all." She folded her arms tightly in front of her. "Can you fix the fence?"

"Yes, Cabe and I will get Brady and Elvin to help. Hopefully, we can get it repaired before it's too dark to work. But it's going to take us well into the evening." He told her the location of the fencing in case she needed to reach them. "Don't hesitate to call if anything comes up."

Gunner tried to run by. Jace scooped him up for a hug before setting him back down again.

"Jace? Should we be worried someone is still on the property?"

Her obvious trust in him didn't go unnoticed. "There's every reason to think this was something random and whoever did it is far away from here now. But I'd still like to be temporarily cautious anyway."

The instinct to reach out and squeeze her hand took him by surprise. He'd originally balked at the idea of Bonnie living nearby for this reason, and his worry that he might not be able to keep his personal and private life separate seemed a valid one.

Right now, though, standing in the room with both Gunner and Bonnie, he was okay with the way things were. Because in this moment, he knew they were safe, and he was close enough to keep it that way.

"Noel should be here between five-thirty and six. But if you wouldn't mind sticking around, I'll make sure you get home okay tonight. I'll pay you time and a half."

A small smile graced her lips as she took a step closer. "No need. I'd enjoy the chance to visit with your sister. Honestly, sometimes the evenings drag out a bit." She shrugged. "It will be a welcome change."

"I'm glad." He smiled at her. "Okay, I'd better get back out there."

Bonnie called Gunner over and reached for his hand. "Come on, big guy. Let's walk your daddy downstairs and then lock the door behind him."

She and Gunner went downstairs ahead of him. Jace grinned as Gunner tried to jump down two steps at a time while Bonnie gripped his hand to keep him from stumbling.

He gave Gunner a hug and kiss. "Be good for Miss Bonnie. I'm going to try real hard to be back before you go to bed."

Gunner put his little arms around Jace's neck and squeezed tight.

Jace set him down and gave Bonnie one last smile. "Thank you."

With that, he waved and headed back out again.

The thought of coming home tonight to find Bonnie still in his house appealed to Jace way more than it should.

"He says it's still going to be a while." Noel shoved her phone into the back pocket of her jeans.

Bonnie looked at the clock for the tenth time that hour. It was nearly half past six. "I hate to eat without him." And unless Cabe took something out there, the guys didn't have anything to eat for dinner, either.

Noel appeared to be thinking along the same lines. "What if we made sandwiches and took food to them? Jace told you where they'd be, right?"

"Yes, and that's a great idea. It'll give Gunner a chance to see his dad before bed, too."

The women smiled at each other, snagged Gunner, and headed for the kitchen. It took them a while to make enough sandwiches for the four men as well as themselves. Forty minutes later, they were in Noel's car. It wasn't hard to locate Jace and the guys.

The men were busy working on the fencing but paused the moment the car came into view. Noel waved.

Bonnie tried to ignore the flutters in her stomach at the sight of Jace. The truth was, she'd seldom thought about Lew since their break-up. But Jace? That was a whole different matter. Thoughts of him filled way more of her waking hours than they ought to.

They got out of the car. "We thought we'd bring you guys some food. I hope you don't mind," Bonnie explained as she helped Gunner out of his car seat.

Noel retrieved two large blankets from the trunk. After spreading them out on the ground, she got the cooler they'd packed.

The men quickly abandoned the fencing in favor of food. Bonnie hadn't met everyone yet, and Jace made the introductions. She shook Cabe's hand and instantly liked the older gentleman. Brady tipped his hat politely while Elvin only stared at her curiously. When he realized she'd seen him, he blinked and looked away.

Everyone was hungry, and it wasn't long before they were all seated on the blankets.

Bonnie thought they would be plenty big enough, but that proved to barely be the case.

She sat first to help unpack the simple dinner. Jace chose a spot next to her, their knees a mere inch from touching each other. If it were possible, she could have sworn there was an electrical current jumping that small gap.

She busied herself handing out food and did her best to ignore Jace's close proximity.

Noel pointed to the fence. "How's it going?"

"We're getting there," Cabe replied. "It took longer than I would've liked to get the panels. It's just a good thing we didn't lose any sheep. They were in a different field." He motioned around their small group. "With the four of us working on the fence, we should have it finished soon."

Jace had mentioned the different fields earlier.

Bonnie had been wondering about the logistics behind where the sheep were placed. "How do you decide which sheep go into which fields?"

Jace swallowed his bite of sandwich before answering. "We keep the ewes and lambs in one field together close to the barn. Older lambs are separated by gender and placed in separate fields. Then we have several sections we use when it comes time to breed the sheep."

"A lot of the time we rotate, too," Cabe added. "It's better for the crops that way."

That made sense. "So you've had the flock in this field before, then?" Bonnie could tell which of the replaced panels were new. The hole in the fence looked to have been a substantial one.

"Yep." Jace brushed his hands off on his jeans. "Which is why it's such a blessing that wasn't the case this time."

They all ate the sandwiches and cookies. Soon afterward, Cabe and the other two men went back to work on the fence. Jace joined him, taking Gunner along.

Bonnie watched as Jace patiently showed Gunner how to use the hammer and then helped the little boy try it himself. Gunner listened attentively and then put his all into the attempt.

"He's an amazing dad," Noel said as she began to put everything back in the cooler. "I wholly credit Grandpa for that, and Jace's determination, because our own father sure wasn't a good example."

There was no missing the bitterness in Noel's voice. Bonnie could certainly sympathize. "Yeah, my parents were never the hands-on type, either. Sometimes, though, having that kind of influence makes us want to do better."

Noel nodded thoughtfully. "I'm sure that's true. It just makes me happy that Gunner has a dad that cares so much about him."

"What was Gunner's mom like?" The question was out of Bonnie's mouth before she realized it. Immediately, she wished she could take it back.

While Noel looked a little surprised, she didn't miss a beat in answering. "Samantha was quiet. Sweet. But she had a lot of walls that made it hard to get to know her. She was that way with Jace even after they got married." She got a faraway look on her face. "Their marriage was almost one of convenience. I know they cared a lot about each other, but I'm not sure they were ever in love. I don't think they realized that until later, either." As though she might have said too much, Noel focused her attention on Jace and Gunner in the distance.

Her voice sad, Noel continued. "Samantha died of an embolism just a few days after Gunner was born. It was such a shock for everyone. She adored Gunner. She would've been a great mom." She sighed, looked at Bonnie, and smiled again. "That's why it makes me happy that Gunner has you, too."

"Me? I'm just the nanny."

"No, you're much more than that." She picked up one side of the blanket and waited for Bonnie to pick up the other. "You're standing in as the mother figure for Gunner."

Bonnie wanted to argue, but Noel wasn't wrong, at least when it came to how much time she spent with the little boy.

The women finished folding the blankets and put them, along with the cooler, in the back of the car.

After closing the trunk, Noel nodded toward the guys. "He cares about you, you know."

Bonnie focused on Gunner as he lost interest in the hammer and started to climb the fence. Jace kept one hand behind his son's back in case he fell.

"Gunner's an amazing kid. When Jace first talked about

moving, the thought of not seeing Gunner anymore broke my heart." Her stomach twisted into knots.

Noel chuckled. "I was talking about my brother."

Bonnie's eyes widened. "I get along with him, and he clearly trusts me with his son. But I doubt…"

Jace had picked up Gunner and swung the boy up onto his shoulders. He headed in their direction.

Noel bumped into Bonnie's arm with her own. "Trust me. I have never seen him look at a woman the way he steals glances at you. And that includes Samantha."

Noel's words crowded Bonnie's brain as Jace approached. He put Gunner back on the ground. "You three should head back to the house. It'll hopefully only be another couple of hours. If it's any longer, I'll let you know." He bent down and kissed his son on the head. "Please text me and let me know when you get there."

That last request was aimed directly at Bonnie. He held her gaze for a moment before smiling at his sister and getting back to work.

His concern was sweet. She tried not to read anything into the request that wasn't there. Of course, he would ask Bonnie instead of Noel to text him. Bonnie normally cared for Gunner, and Jace would want to know his son was home safe. There was nothing more to it than that. But no matter how hard she tried, she couldn't shut out what Noel said about Jace caring about her or the hope it ignited in her heart.

Chapter Nine

Bonnie scraped carrots and potatoes off the cutting board with a knife and into the bottom of the slow cooker. She added a little water then placed a large roast on top. After sprinkling some herbs and spices, she put the lid on and set it to low.

The meal would be done by dinner. Bonnie knew Jace generally didn't want her to do any cooking for him, but Noel had hinted at the roast in the fridge. It's not like it took that much to put it all in the slow cooker anyway.

She thought over the last couple of days since the fence had been damaged. Thankfully, Jace and the guys got it repaired. Maybe Jace's thoughts on it being a random event were right on the money because nothing else had happened.

Nothing at all. On any front.

After Noel's insinuation that Jace cared more for her than just a nanny for his son, Bonnie had been hyper-aware of everything he did or said. But if he was attracted to her, he sure was good at hiding it.

Which meant, either way, she needed to bury her own feelings down so far even she forgot they were there. Besides, for all she knew, he was still mourning his wife and Noel was completely off her rocker.

Bonnie looked down at Gunner. "What do you say we bake some cookies today?"

The boy's eyes brightened. "Cookies!"

It wasn't even lunch yet, and the day had dragged on for what seemed like forever. Baking some cookies would help take up a little time.

Bonnie had just retrieved all the ingredients from the cupboards and set the oven to preheat when the doorbell rang.

"Who could that be?" she asked Gunner. "Come on, let's go answer the door."

A peek through the peephole revealed a woman Bonnie didn't recognize. She opened the door to find the woman donning impeccable clothing along with an impenetrable expression.

"Can I help you?"

"You must be the nanny." The woman tried to push her way past Bonnie.

With one hand on the door and the other against the door-frame, Bonnie blocked her way. The woman's dismissive nature immediately had Bonnie's hackles up. "I don't believe we've been introduced. My name is Bonnie Tabor. Who might you be?"

The woman stared daggers at Bonnie. "I'm Mrs. Leslie Echolls, and Jace is my son. I expect you to let me in this instant."

Bonnie's mind raced. She could see the similarity between this woman and both Jace and Noel–especially in the eyes. If Bonnie turned Mrs. Echolls away, would Jace be upset?

"Why don't you come in, Mrs. Echolls." Bonnie stepped to the side. "If you'll have a seat in the living room, I'll let Jace know you're here. Would you like some iced tea?"

Mrs. Echolls lifted her chin and straightened her spine. Everything about her oozed confidence and determination. "I'm not here to speak with Jace. I thought I might have a word with you." She turned and raised a well-manicured eyebrow. "I'd appreciate it if you'd allow us to have our conversation first before letting my son know I'm here."

Bonnie wasn't at all comfortable with this. But until she had an idea of what it was Mrs. Echolls wanted to talk about, there wasn't any harm in waiting things out. At least for a few minutes. She could always text Jace anytime.

"Sure. Give me a moment, please." She waited long enough to wait for Mrs. Echolls to sit down before going back into the kitchen. She put the cookie dough in the fridge, turned off the stove, and led Gunner into the living room.

She wasn't sure what she expected from Mrs. Echolls when it came to seeing her grandson, but indifference with a tinge of disdain wasn't it.

There was no real interest from Gunner, either. The little boy was starting to look sleepy. She picked him up and settled in the recliner where she slowly rocked it back and forth. "What did you want to see me about, Mrs. Echolls?"

The older woman's gaze stalled on Gunner. "Shouldn't you put him down for a nap or something?"

Bonnie had to physically bite her tongue to keep from saying something she shouldn't. What kind of grandparent didn't want anything to do with her grandchild?

She hugged Gunner close, willing him to feel the love she had for him. "It's not quite his naptime yet. In fact, we were about to make some cookies. Weren't we, buddy?"

Gunner nodded enthusiastically. "Cookies!" As though he sensed the unease in the room, he tucked his head into Bonnie's shoulder and remained on her lap.

"Very well." Mrs. Echolls straightened her blouse and primly crossed her legs. "I want you to convince Jace that his son would be better off back in Clearwater. He needs to sell this ranch and go back to working for his father's company. Walking away from his position and the money it entailed was foolhardy. He could be providing more than this," she waved her arms around, "for his son." With that, she folded her hands on her lap and leveled Bonnie with a stare full of judgment.

Bonnie waited, half expecting her to say something else or even insinuate that she was joking. Bonnie didn't know much about Jace's financial status. What she did know was how much he loved his son, and that no one had a right to question that. Jace had been more relaxed after moving than she'd ever known him to be.

"Jace feels that this is the right place to raise Gunner. Neither of us can make that decision as well as Jace can."

Mrs. Echolls eyes flashed. "Do you have children?"

Bonnie clenched her jaw. "No, ma'am, I don't."

"Then you cannot pretend to know what it's like to raise one. My son should not be toiling away on a ranch when he could be next in line to run our family's company." She brushed at something invisible on her dress, clearly agitated. "He should enroll the child in boarding school and be done with it. Not hide him away in the country with a half-wit of a nanny because of some misplaced sense of obligation. Jace is ruining his life, and by working for him, you are enabling that."

Bonnie stared at Mrs. Echolls in disbelief. "A boarding school for a toddler? I didn't even realize there was such a thing." How dumb did the woman think Bonnie was? She looked down at the little boy in her arms. Bonnie was thankful he'd fallen asleep, completely unaware of the poisonous words being spewed around him.

Looking at his sweet, innocent face, however, was all she needed to strengthen her resolve. This might not be her house, but she was in charge of Gunner. It was her responsibility to ensure his emotional and physical well-being. Right now, that meant not allowing a clearly hateful individual to have an influence on him.

She scooped Gunner into her arms as she stood. "Mrs. Echolls, I'd appreciate it if you'd leave the house now. I have heard enough. I'll thank you to call ahead next time you come. That way Jace will be here to greet you, and I can have refreshments ready."

Bonnie was proud of herself for not saying what was on her mind, even if the tone of her voice didn't quite match the congeniality of her words.

Mrs. Echolls face turned red and she pinched her lips together as though ready to argue. Instead, she stood, rod straight, and made her way to the front door.

Once there, she whirled back around. "If you truly care about the well-being of that child, you'll encourage Jace to move back into town and go back to working with his father."

Mrs. Echolls was halfway to her car when Jace's truck stopped in the driveway. He got out and strode toward his mom, his expression blank.

As they spoke, Bonnie imagined how Mrs. Echolls was telling him about Bonnie being inhospitable and throwing her out of the house.

Bonnie tried to be polite. But throw Mrs. Echolls out of Jace's house? Yeah, she'd done that. Ugh, she should've just gone with her initial instinct and texted him to let him know his mother was here. At least then a lot of the pressure would've been off of Bonnie.

Jace's gaze strayed from his mother to the front door where he clearly saw her watching them.

Bonnie wished she could tell what they were talking about.

One thing was certain: Jace could be as angry at her as he

wanted to be, but if she had to handle it all over again, Bonnie would do nothing differently.

To her relief, Mrs. Echolls got into her car and drove away. Moments later, Jace approached the front door and stepped inside. "I saw her car on the way by. It sounds like I was a little late to the party."

There was no missing the tension in his tone.

Bonnie fully expected to be reprimanded for the way she handled the situation. But it wasn't going to happen with Gunner in her arms.

"I was just about to put Gunner down for a nap." She shifted his weight, amazed at how heavy a sleeping little boy could get.

"Here, I'll take him for you." Jace easily lifted Gunner into his arms. "I'll be right back."

Bonnie inhaled deeply as the lingering scent of Jace's aftershave remained behind.

Well, no matter what Jace had to say, there was no way she was going to apologize for what she said to that hateful woman. She just hoped she still had a job when it was all said and done.

§

THE MOMENT JACE SAW HIS MOTHER'S CAR PARKED IN FRONT of the house, all of the tension he'd left behind when he quit his job and moved to the ranch slammed into his chest. What made her think it was okay to just show up here? She hadn't so much as spoken to him or Noel since they told her of their plans to keep the ranch.

Jace tried to call them once and had to leave a message. They never returned the call, and he'd taken his cue from them and didn't mess with it again. But Noel had tried multiple times to reach out, only to be ignored.

It'd been clear when he met Mother in the driveway that she hadn't expected him, which only annoyed him further. Then seeing Bonnie standing in the door, Gunner in her arms, kicked his instincts to protect them into high gear.

Since Mother refused to tell him why she'd come, he'd feigned a polite demeanor and asked her to please call ahead next time so he could make sure he was home for the visit. It only seemed to annoy her as she got into her car and left.

Jace ascended the stairs, his sleeping son nestled against his chest, and wondered what all his mother might have said to Bonnie.

He remembered well the harsh words his mother had easily dished out to the people she employed. If she said anything inappropriate to Bonnie or Gunner…

He gently got Gunner settled in his bed. The moment the boy's head touched his pillow, he released a deep sigh. Jace loved it when he sighed like that. Oh, to sleep the sleep of an innocent child.

He stayed several moments and prayed for his son before going back downstairs. He needed to talk to Bonnie and find out what his mother said to her.

Jace didn't expect to find Bonnie waiting for him at the base of the stairs, her fists on her hips, and fire burning in her eyes. She didn't give him a chance to speak first.

"I refuse to apologize, Jace. I tried to be hospitable. I offered to call you, but she asked me not to. I stayed quiet for as long as I could." She paced away from him and back again.

He had no doubt that was true. In the time he'd known her, he had never seen her conduct herself in any way other than professional. Even when they argued about something. He had no reason to believe that wasn't the case today. "What–"

"I saw you talking to her outside. I'm sure she told you all about how I threw her out of the house…"

Jace's jaw dropped. "You threw my mother out?"

"Well, I asked her to leave. But basically, yeah." Bonnie's cheeks betrayed her embarrassment as she used her hands to comb through her hair. Several strands stuck out behind one ear. "I know I didn't have the right, and that this is your house."

"You're right, it is my house." And as far as he was concerned, Bonnie had more of a right to be in it than his own mother did.

"I would've been fine if she'd only had things to say about me. But the moment she brought Gunner into it…"

The anger Jace had tried his best to force down flared up like gasoline on a forest fire. "What did she say?" Bonnie bit her bottom lip and hesitated. He took several steps closer, the toes of their shoes nearly touching. "Bonnie, tell me what she said."

"She called Gunner an obligation and said you were ruining your life." Her right hand grasped her left arm and she squeezed hard enough to turn the skin around her fingers white. "She said that Gunner should be put in a boarding school and that you needed to go back to working for your father."

It wasn't anything his mother hadn't said to him already. But that she would continue to insist on it and drag Bonnie into the mix was inexcusable. When his hand started to ache, he realized his fists were clenched. "And what did she say about you?"

"That doesn't matter."

"Yes, Bonnie, it does." It mattered a great deal, and if he knew his mother at all, it couldn't have been nice.

Bonnie let her hands fall to her sides. For the first time

since he'd gotten home, her gaze dropped from his face to the wall behind him, their shoes, and even the window nearby.

"She said that, since I wasn't a parent, I wasn't fit to care for Gunner. That I was a half-wit who was only enabling your choice to stay out here."

Jace clenched his jaw as he drew in a breath and let it back out again.

Bonnie crossed her arms in front of her. Her beautiful brown eyes swirled with a combination of determination and uncertainty. "I don't understand why she felt the need to speak with me instead of coming to you directly. I wish I'd let you know immediately that she'd stopped by, but like I said earlier, I won't apologize for asking her to leave."

She clearly expected him to disagree with how she'd handled the situation. Nothing could be further from the truth. "Bonnie?" She watched him expectantly. "Thank you."

She blinked at him as though she couldn't believe what she was hearing. "What?"

"Thank you. For not letting her bully you. For kicking her out of my house. And especially for standing up for my son." He smiled as she released a lungful of air and let her hands fall to her sides.

"Then you're not going to fire me."

"Are you kidding? I'm inclined to give you a raise." The wayward strands of hair caught his eye. Without a second thought, he reached out and tucked them behind her ear. "For the record, your care of Gunner has proven that you would be an infinitely better mother to your own children than mine ever was to Noel and me." He let his hand linger near her ear for far longer than he should have.

Only now did he realize just how close they were standing to each other. He caught a hint of her fruity shampoo and forced himself to take a step back.

For the first time, Bonnie's eyes got misty as she blinked

away the tears. "Thank you," she said, her voice just above a whisper. She shook her head. "I don't know how anyone can treat their grandson like that. She never even told Gunner hello." Her voice caught. "To insinuate he was a burden…"

Jace had made it a point not to tell Bonnie about the past. He stood by that decision—until now. If Mother was going to pull Bonnie into the family's mess, Bonnie deserved to know what would inevitably be dredged up. It was better she hear it from him…

Chapter Ten

❧

Bonnie accepted the bottle of soda Jace handed her and followed him to the porch swing outside. He set the baby monitor down on the rail and took a seat, motioning for Bonnie to join him.

The swing shifted beneath her as she got settled. She twisted the cap off her cola and took a sip, the bubbles tickling her throat on the way down.

How was she supposed to wrap her head around what happened? One minute she was throwing Mrs. Echolls out of the house and the next she was sure Jace was going to fire her.

What she hadn't expected was for him to thank her for what she did. And the way he tucked her hair behind her ear... It'd been tender. Thoughtful. Was he simply relieved that she hadn't sided with his mother, or could Noel at least be partially right?

Her throat suddenly dry, Bonnie took another big swallow of her soda.

In the time she'd worked for Jace, she'd had a lot of questions about his past, Gunner's mom, and a million other things. Noel had helped with some of it, but Mrs. Echolls visit brought up even more. Normally, she'd keep them to herself because it wasn't her business.

But now…Well, now Mrs. Echolls had brought her into the midst of it. Bonnie had the right to ask a few questions even though she wasn't sure Jace was going to answer.

She cleared her throat and clutched her soda bottle with both hands. "Jace? Why does your mother consider Gunner a burden?"

Jace released a heavy sigh and leaned back against the swing. "My wife and I knew each other for a while, but really only dated a few months before we got married. Samantha was in a financial crisis, and my parents didn't approve of her." He paused and stared at the bottle in his hand. "Even after we were married, my parents were nothing but rude. They never accepted her. They accused her of wanting to marry me with the goal of leaving at some point with half of my money. They insisted she had no interest in me personally, and that I needed to protect the family fortune. I'm sad to say the fact that they were so against her was a big incentive for me."

After today, it wasn't hard for Bonnie to imagine Jace pushing the boundaries his parents might have laid out for him.

Jace continued. "Well, I'll never tell this to my parents, but they were right about some things. Samantha and I barely knew each other, and that was only magnified later after we were married." He paused and swallowed hard. "My parents always thought Samantha and I could get a divorce and go our separate ways at some point. And then Gunner came along. Instead of being happy about a grandchild, they saw it as a chain that would forever link me with Samantha." He released a slow breath. "Noel mentioned she told you what happened to Samantha." He waited for Bonnie to nod and then continued. "She didn't have any family. After she died, my parents thought I should consider placing Gunner up for adoption and get my life back."

"What?" Bonnie's mind struggled to comprehend how anyone could suggest such a thing. Not only were they willing to give their grandchild away, but Jace had just lost his wife. "How could they…. Poor Gunner." And poor Jace, too. She couldn't even begin to imagine the storm of emotions he must have gone through. "I don't understand how they could dismiss their own grandchild like that."

"I don't either. But you know, I've come to realize that, if they're going to act like that, then I'd rather they weren't around him." He waved a hand toward the driveway. "You saw how my mother was with him. She thinks raising a son and being a single dad is going to ruin my life. I suppose that's a good indication of how my parents feel about having children, huh?" His voice dripped with sarcasm.

Several choice words went through Bonnie's mind. How could two people like Jace's parents be so horrible? Clearly they'd never gotten to know their own son, or they would see how much they had to be proud of.

Her eyes stung with unshed tears over the horrible injustice of it all.

"They don't deserve Gunner." That, she knew with all of her being. She raised her chin and waited until Jace was looking at her. "Your parents are fools. If they don't look at you and lose count of the reasons why they should be proud you are their son, then they don't deserve you, either. Don't ever doubt what you're doing. You're an amazing dad."

She started to reach out and touch his forearm but halted the movement. He glanced at her hand and then at her face, letting her know that he'd noticed.

Bonnie shifted her weight to lean into the corner of the porch swing a little further away from Jace. She struggled to refocus their conversation. "So why is your mother against you living here at the ranch if she has nothing to do with Gunner anyway?"

Jace barked out a laugh. "When Grandpa died, my parents had every intention of selling this place. The land is worth a small fortune—as if my parents don't have enough money." He shook his head. "When Grandpa left the ranch to Noel and me in the will, my parents were furious. They think it should be sold and split four ways with my mother and father each getting one of the shares."

Bonnie didn't know what to say to that. That someone would be so money-hungry... She knew Jace must have a fair amount of money himself, but at least he didn't act like it.

"Well, I never met your grandpa, but I'm sure I would've liked him. And I have no doubt he would be happy that you, Noel, and Gunner are living here now."

Jace remained silent. When Bonnie tilted her head to look at him, she found him watching her. She couldn't quite decipher the expression on his face, but she wasn't sure she'd seen it before.

"So what about you?" Jace gave her a small smile. "Are you close with your parents?"

Bonnie immediately made a face and then laughed. "Not particularly. My parents have a lot of money and had an inheritance set aside for my sisters, brother, and me. Originally, we just had to wait until we were twenty-one to get it. Then my oldest sister got there first."

It'd been years ago, but the drama of it all felt like yesterday. "She took her money, toured the world, and came back nearly broke two years later. She's spent the last sixteen years married to a man that didn't have nearly as much money as she'd like him to have. To say my parents were less than thrilled is an understatement."

"Let me guess, they took it out on the rest of you."

"To a degree. They changed the stipulations to where we

got the money if we stayed connected to the family business in one way or another, were twenty-five, and married. They said it was to make sure our lives were stable. After everything that happened with Violet, my other sister, Lucy, followed their guidelines."

"But you haven't." Jace chuckled. "You don't seem like the type to follow rules like that."

Bonnie feigned offense but couldn't keep the smile off her face. "You're right, and neither is my brother. Wyatt quit the family business when he opened up Joyful Hope Stables. And me…" Her voice trailed off.

Jace tapped her knee with his. "What about you?"

"I'm thirty-one, unmarried, and I work as a nanny. As far as my parents are concerned, I'm the very definition of a failure." She tried to keep her tone light as though it didn't matter. Because, truthfully, she wouldn't change a thing about her life. But her parents' opinion of her still stung. She supposed it probably felt that way to Jace, too. "My mom, especially, puts a lot of importance on money and a rich husband. She likes to tell me often that I should be the one hiring a nanny for my children, not working as the hired help myself." She pinched the bridge of her nose. "Sorry. I hope you know that's not the way I feel."

She loved everything about her job as Gunner's nanny. But her mom had frequently reminded her that she would never find a man to marry her as long as she worked as a nanny for a single dad, and Bonnie sometimes wondered if she was right, even if the risk was worth it to her.

HEARING ABOUT HOW BONNIE'S PARENTS TREATED HER MADE Jace angry on a personal level. He'd had to go through a lot with his own parents. Now talking to Bonnie just reinforced how desperately he wanted things to be different for Gunner. To stop this cycle before it could continue. He wanted his son to know that Jace enjoyed being a parent and that Gunner was a true blessing in his life.

As far as Bonnie went, he didn't understand how she was still single. Any guy who met her and didn't snatch her up was insane.

Except there was a small part of him that was glad that hadn't happened yet. Picturing Bonnie in the arms of another man kicked jealously into high gear, and that was an emotion he had no right to.

She deserved love. Happiness. She deserved a doting husband who saw how amazing she was, and a houseful of her own children, if that's what she wanted.

So why was he picturing her in his house? Why could he suddenly imagine Gunner playing with a little sister who looked a lot like Bonnie?

He watched Bonnie sitting on the porch swing beside him and the need to pull her into his arms and kiss her was nearly overwhelming.

Jace cleared his throat and stood to put some distance between himself and Bonnie before he followed his instincts and messed everything up.

Bonnie must have taken his thoughtful silence for uncertainty. She stood and Jace reached for her hands. Bonnie stilled the moment they touched.

"Your parents are idiots if they don't get how amazing their daughter is." Jace's words were firm, and he meant every syllable of them. "The right guy is going to come along, Bonnie. And when he does, he'll be a fool if he doesn't do everything in his power to make you the happiest woman on the planet."

"Thanks," Bonnie spoke just above a whisper. She pulled her hands away and stood still. She didn't quite meet his eyes.

"I'd better go get a few things done before Gunner wakes from his nap."

She turned and went inside, leaving Jace wondering whether he'd said something to hurt her. Unable to just leave it like it was, he followed her.

"Bonnie? Did I say something wrong?"

"No." The tone of her voice was anything but convincing. However, the expression on her face clearly said she didn't want to talk about it. "I need to check on the roast." She paused. "Noel asked if I would put it on for tonight. I hope you don't mind."

He'd always made a big deal of Bonnie not cooking for him. Now, seeing her hesitation, he regretted being so rigid about it.

"Of course not. But I hope you'll stay and have dinner with us."

Bonnie slowly shook her head. "That's not a good idea, Jace. I should go home. You've always made it clear you value your personal life. I have no wish to intrude on that."

Jace's eyebrows drew together. She was right. But right now, even though it made no sense, and he should be squelching those instincts, he needed her to be a bigger part of his life.

But how did he change that? How did he show her that she didn't have to vacate the area every time he walked in?

"Look, you had to deal with a lot when my mother was here. The least we can do is invite you to share a meal with us in thanks. Please. I know Noel would agree with me."

She shook her head and pressed her lips together for a moment. "I can't. I promised my brother I'd stop by this evening."

There was little Jace could say to that. He bit his tongue to keep from telling her to be careful or to text him when she got home.

Instead, he simply nodded, offered her a friendly smile, and said, "I hope you have a good visit. Thanks again for what you did with my mother. I appreciate it."

"You're welcome, Jace."

With that, he left. But his mind never strayed far from Bonnie or their conversation.

Chapter Eleven

Wyatt opened the front door and ushered Bonnie inside. As soon as Jace had left the house again earlier, she'd texted Wyatt to ask if she could bring dinner by. That way at least she hadn't totally lied to Jace about having other plans.

Thankfully, Chrissy was starting to feel a little better, and both she and Wyatt said Bonnie was more than welcome to come over.

Especially, as Wyatt mentioned, if Bonnie was bringing the food.

She set the takeout bags down on the kitchen table then turned to give her brother and sister-in-law hugs. "Thanks for letting me crash this evening, guys. I promise I won't stay long." She pointed to the bags. "I brought chicken, mashed potatoes, and gravy. I hope that sounds okay."

"Are you kidding?" Chrissy started to unpack the bags. "I'm practically living on mashed potatoes right now. Apparently, this baby is quite the fan." She patted her still-flat tummy.

Wyatt chuckled. "You've made my wife's day." He wrapped an arm around Bonnie's shoulders. "We're happy to have you here anytime, but I have a feeling there's something else going on. Do you want to talk about it?"

Chrissy shot her husband a look. "Let's at least get dinner on the table before it gets cold. Poor Bonnie barely stepped in the house."

Bonnie nudged Chrissy with her arm. "Thanks, sis." She stuck her tongue out at Wyatt then helped Chrissy get everything out.

After praying over the food, they started to eat. Except about all Bonnie could do was take a bite of potatoes as she tried to choose her words. She groaned. Wyatt was going to enjoy this way too much.

She wiped her hands on a napkin and sighed. "I'm falling for my boss." She pointed a finger at Wyatt. "And if you say 'I told you so' to me, I'll throw my chicken at you."

Chrissy stopped eating, a roll in her hand, and glanced from Bonnie to Wyatt.

At least Wyatt had the good sense not to look smug. "You're serious."

"I wish I weren't." It would be much easier that way.

"Are you in love with him?" The question came from Chrissy.

"I'm not sure. Maybe. I mean, if I was, I'd know, right?" If she weren't in love with the guy, there was still hope she could get rid of these ridiculous notions. Take their relationship—at least her perception of it—back to normal before she did something stupid to jeopardize her job.

"Sometimes love sneaks up on you when you least expect it." Wyatt shared a knowing look with Chrissy. "How does Jace feel about you?"

"He's always seen me as an employee. He treats me well and is more than fair. But today we were talking after I threw his mother out of the house, and I think something's shifting. He at least wants to be friends." Bonnie stirred her mashed potatoes and gravy together. "I would like that, too. But I'm not sure it's such a good idea." She let the fork fall to her plate.

Wyatt held up a hand. "Wait a minute. You threw his mother out of the house?"

Chrissy held a napkin over her mouth as she frantically tried to finish her bite of food. "Okay, you're going to have to start from the beginning."

They ate while Bonnie told them the story about Mrs. Echolls, the horrible things she said, and then about Bonnie's conversation with Jace afterward. She left out the way he'd held her hands because she didn't want that to skew Wyatt's or Chrissy's opinion.

Bonnie swore she could still feel his skin against hers.

"He invited you to stay for dinner tonight, and that's why you think he has feelings for you?" Wyatt's face was serious, but the tone of his voice gave him away.

Bonnie threw a roll at him. "Funny. When you say it that way, it makes me sound like a ninny."

Chrissy ignored them both. "It does sound like he's holding out an olive branch." Chrissy spooned some more mashed potatoes onto her plate. "The question is, if you found out he was falling in love with you, how would you feel?"

"I don't know." Bonnie groaned. "What if it didn't work out? I'd be out of a job and wouldn't see Gunner again. What if he's still mourning his wife? Plus, I'd be jumping into another messed-up family with money issues. Who needs that? I walked away from our family's money and swore I didn't need anyone else's." She groaned. "Mom would have all kinds of things to say if I ended up marrying a rich man. She'd tell me it could've happened earlier if I'd only listened to her and would never let me forget it." That last part made her shudder. "Very little good can come from any of this."

Chrissy rested her chin in the palm of her hand. "Unless he's the love of your life." She raised an eyebrow.

"Sure, there's that." Bonnie stabbed a piece of chicken with her fork and shoved it into her mouth. "So what am I supposed to do?"

Wyatt thought for several moments. "You know what Gran would say, right?"

Bonnie leaned into the back of her chair. "Pray about it, and everything will work itself out."

"Sounds like good advice to me." Wyatt winked. "Does he go to church? If not, you could invite him to join us one Sunday."

"You don't think that's too forward?"

Chrissy shook her head. "Not if you invite both him and Noel."

"Exactly," Wyatt agreed. "Put the ball in his court, so to speak." He pointed a finger at her. "Just let me know if he treats you wrong. I'm serious about that."

Wyatt was smiling, but Bonnie knew he'd be there for her if she ever needed him. She'd always been able to rely on her brother. "I appreciate it."

She finally took another bite of her cold mashed potatoes.

She could pray. Maybe invite Jace and Noel to church. And then wait. She had no intention of quitting her job, and Jace wasn't going anywhere.

Maybe it was best to just continue like she always had. Maybe the change she was seeing in Jace was all in her head. Or maybe he did just want to be friends. Whatever the case may be, she'd have to take the wait and see approach.

Totally not her cup of tea.

"I WISH I'D BEEN THERE TO SEE HER FACE WHEN BONNIE

asked her to leave." Just the thought of it had Jace grinning ear to ear.

Noel tapped her meal with her fork. "Yep. Between that and this amazing roast, Bonnie may officially be my hero. I kind of wish I were a fly on the wall in Mom and Dad's house tonight."

"Me, too." Jace took a bite of his roast. It was some of the best he'd ever tasted. Bonnie crossed his mind, and he wished she'd taken him up on his offer to eat with them.

He wanted to regret spilling his guts to her about his family and about what happened with Samantha, but he couldn't. He'd spent the last year and a half keeping everything personal from Bonnie. Telling her had been therapeutic in a lot of ways.

The best part was having the chance to learn more about her. He was quickly discovering that spending time with her was highly addicting.

Which brought Jace back to wishing she were here with them tonight. Yet, after he'd drilled it into her that she shouldn't have anything to do with his evening meals, how could he blame her for not?

Gunner finished his helping of potatoes but hadn't touched much of his roast. The kiddo never did care much for meat, though, unless it was chicken.

Jace warmed up three chicken nuggets and handed them to his eager son.

They finished their evening meal. Jace bathed his son, they played for a while, and then Jace got the sleepy little guy down for the night.

After tucking him in, Jace glanced out an upstairs window, relieved to spot her car in the driveway. Truthfully, the turn into the ranch could be difficult to see at night, and he hated the idea of her driving around out there unable to find it.

He withdrew his phone and sent her a text. "Noel and I enjoyed the roast. It was amazing. Thanks again for having that ready this evening. I hope you had a good visit with your family."

He looked outside again, imagining her hearing the ping of his text and swiping her phone's screen to read it.

Moments later, his phone announced a reply.

Jace smiled as he read it.

"I'm glad you enjoyed it. Yes, I had a good time. It was just what I needed."

He wanted to keep chatting with her but didn't know what to say. Instead, he typed, "I'm glad. Have a good night, Bonnie."

There was no response at first. Jace headed back downstairs again. Just as he reached the landing, the welcome ping sounded.

"You, too."

JACE WAS HIKING IN THE MOUNTAINS AND COULDN'T FIGURE out where the strange chime was coming from. It wasn't until the mountain range faded into the familiar surroundings of his bedroom that he realized it was his phone ringing.

He sat up in bed, turned the nearby lamp on, and reached for the offending device. It was just after four in the morning. As soon as he saw it was Bonnie calling, he swiped to answer it. "Hey. Everything okay?" His voice sounded deeper and gravel-filled even to his own ears. He cleared his throat.

"Jace?" Her voice was a harsh whisper. "It sounds like someone is downstairs in the garage. It isn't you, is it?"

"No." He couldn't remember actually getting out of bed. He pulled a pair of jeans on while holding the phone to his ear with his shoulder. "Is your door locked?"

"Yes. And I moved a chair in front of it, too."

"Okay, good. Stay there. I'll check it out." With that, he ended the call, pulled a t-shirt on over his head, and slid his feet into his boots. Next, he opened the gun safe on the side table and quickly slid his handgun into the leather holster at his hip before jogging downstairs.

He met Noel in the living room. She had her arms folded as she stifled a yawn. "What's wrong? I could hear you stomping around up there like a herd of elephants."

"Bonnie called and said someone's in the garage. I'm going to head over and check it out." He sent a text to see if Cabe was up and around the ranch. "Lock the door behind me," he instructed his sister.

Noel nodded. "Be careful."

"I will. Be back in a few minutes."

Jace's phone buzzed. He glanced at it to read Cabe's response. "Hang tight, I'll meet you there."

Normally, Jace would wait for Cabe, but not with Bonnie above the garage. With any luck, if someone did break into the garage, they were long gone by now.

He went outside and waited until he heard the door latch behind him before continuing around the front of the house. He'd just reached the side when the sound of a truck approaching stopped him. Cabe jumped out, a smug look on his face. "I knew you wouldn't wait. Definitely Jethro's grand-son." He grabbed a rifle out of the cab of the truck. "Let's go."

Jace nodded his agreement and followed the older man's lead. The door into the garage was open, and the scratches in the wood informed them the lock had been broken. Most likely with a crowbar or something similar.

The men made eye contact. Bonnie was right. Someone was in the garage who wasn't supposed to be there. Now the question remained: Was the intruder still present?

Jace forced himself to breathe evenly to keep his heart rate lower and his focus sharp. Systematically, he and Cabe went through the garage and storage area but found no evidence of the intruder.

Cabe lowered his rifle. "Probably heard my truck when I pulled up to the house."

Hopefully that was the case. On one hand, if the person who broke in was the same person who damaged the fencing, at least they might have caught the guy. On the other, the intruder could've been armed and waiting for them.

He glanced at the stairs leading to Bonnie's apartment.

"Go ahead," Cabe told him. "I'll keep watch down here and call the police."

Jace didn't wait to see if Cabe took out his cell phone. When Jace got to the top of the stairs, he called out, "Bonnie, it's me. We're all clear down here."

The sound of a chair scraping the floor was quickly followed by the deadbolt sliding open. The doorknob twisted and soon he was looking into her dark eyes.

"Oh, thank goodness. I hated to wake you up, but I wasn't sure what else to do." She opened the door all the way and stepped out onto the landing.

Jace took in her baggy shorts and sweatshirt. The look was genuinely adorable on her. "Never hesitate to call. It's good you did, too. Someone broke into the garage. I can't tell yet if anything was taken, but Cabe should be on the phone with the police department now." He realized he was still holding the gun and holstered it.

"Do you think they were after all the tools?"

Jace thought about Grandpa's extensive tool collection downstairs. "That's possible." He made a mental note to take full inventory but they probably stopped the guy before he had a chance to take much. There's no way he could've gotten away with many tools on foot, and he was long gone by the time they got there.

Cabe came up behind them. He put a hand on the receiving end of the phone. "You need to find out if anything has been stolen. If not, we take pictures and file a report online." He turned his attention back to the phone.

Bonnie's eyes widened. "So much for the good old days when the sheriff sent a deputy out to check on things."

"Yep." Jace hesitated. He hated the idea of Bonnie out here with the lock broken on the outer door. "You can stay in the main house for the rest of the night if you'd like."

Bonnie glanced at her watch. "You know, by the time my nerves settle, the sun will be coming up anyway. Give me a few minutes to change, and I'll come down and see if there's anything I can do to help."

He couldn't blame her. It was doubtful he'd be able to go to sleep, either. He called Noel to let her know what was happening and then started to go through the garage with a critical eye.

"Is anything missing?" Bonnie's voice snagged his attention several minutes later.

"Not a thing." Jace frowned. Tonight seemed more of a random and spontaneous event compared to the fencing. Could they be dealing with separate individuals altogether?

The unknown was driving him crazy.

An hour later, Jace finished uploading the police report. Cabe had left some time earlier, and Bonnie was sitting perched on a stool as she covered a yawn.

He offered a sympathetic smile. They would all be dragging today. "I'll have the lock replaced before the end of the day and get you a new key. I'll also have a security camera installed here as well as at both doors in the house."

"That sounds good. Thank you, Jace." She yawned again. "Looks like coffee is in order."

"I'll put a pot on at the house. That way it'll be ready when you get there. And if you need the day off to catch up on some rest, I would certainly understand."

"And miss out on all the excitement around here lately? Not a chance." Bonnie chuckled. "I appreciate it, though." She motioned toward the stairs. "I'm going to go back up. I'm glad none of your grandpa's tools were stolen."

"Thanks, Bonnie. Me, too." He hesitated. "Call if you need anything."

"I will." With a final smile, she turned and went back up the stairs.

Jace heard her door close and lock behind her. Thank God the apartment had its own deadbolt. Still, he shuddered to think about the intruder continuing through the garage and trying to get into Bonnie's apartment.

Yes, a new lock and cameras at all outer doors were a must.

Chapter Twelve

Gunner's cries greeted Bonnie Thursday morning. Usually, when she arrived at the main house, Gunner was happy and excited to see her.

Today, she found Gunner and Jace in the living room. Gunner sat on the floor, back against the couch, with giant tears rolling down his cheeks.

When Jace looked up, he flinched apologetically. "Happy Thursday."

Bonnie could tell this had been going on for some time. She resisted the instinct to reach out and pat his shoulder. "I can see it started off with a bang for you."

Jace raised an eyebrow. "Noel had to leave early this morning, and that threw his schedule off. Then I poured syrup on his pancakes instead of letting him dip them into the syrup himself. I had no idea he even wanted to do that."

Bonnie couldn't recall Gunner eating them, either. "Of all the nerve. Syrup on pancakes. What gave you that idea?" She winked at him.

The poor boy's face was a mess between the streaks of tears and his runny nose. Bonnie got a tissue from a nearby box and sat cross-legged on the floor next to him. "Let's get your face cleaned up. Then how about you help me load the dishwasher. Can you put the forks and spoons into the basket?"

Gunner sniffed and nodded. He squirmed when Bonnie wiped his face then ran his arm across his nose. "Put the 'poons in."

"That's right, you can put the spoons in. Why don't you give Daddy a big hug since he's about to go to work?"

Gunner got to his feet and flung himself at Jace, their hug punctuated by a little hiccup from the boy.

Jace rubbed his son's back. "You be good for Miss Bonnie. I love you, buddy."

"I love you, buddy," Gunner echoed back as he ran to the kitchen.

Bonnie found Jace watching her, admiration shining in his blue eyes. "If you could sell your technique in a bottle, you'd be a wealthy woman."

She laughed loudly at that. "I'm not sure about that. I appreciate your vote of confidence, though." She tilted her head toward the front door. "I've got this. Go wrangle some sheep or whatever it is you do during the day."

Now it was Jace's turn to laugh. "Actually, we've got several ewes that are about ready to have their lambs. Cabe is going to show me the ropes."

Bonnie pictured a newborn lamb and could imagine just how cute it would be. "We'll have to take Gunner out to see one once it's born. I'd like that, too."

He gave a decisive nod. "I'll make sure that happens. Thanks again, Bonnie. You are a lifesaver."

With that, he gave her a final wave and left the house. Bonnie stared at the door long after it had latched until the sound of Gunner trying to open the dishwasher drew her into the kitchen before her young charge made too much of a mess.

By the time lunch came along, it was clear why Gunner had been emotional all morning: He was getting sick. His forehead was warm, but Bonnie didn't have much luck locating the thermometer.

She finally found it in a box underneath the kitchen sink. Apparently, it hadn't been unpacked since the move. The readout confirmed her suspicions. Gunner had a fever of just over one hundred. No wonder he was miserable.

Even though she knew Jace would have no problem with Bonnie giving Gunner some medication, she wanted to text him anyway.

She got a response almost immediately. "Yes, of course. Poor guy. Maybe he's teething."

"I think he's coming down with something. I'll give him some Tylenol and hopefully it'll help. Will keep you updated."

Even though the liquid Tylenol tasted like grape, Gunner acted as though it were vile the way he fought her over swallowing it.

When it was all said and done, Bonnie finally had to carry the boy to the rocking chair in the living room. He cried for some time before he leaned into her, exhausted, and fell asleep.

Bonnie held his little body close. The medication brought the temperature down some, but not as much as she would've liked.

When Gunner began to snore softly, she decided he was out enough for her to get him to his bed. He didn't budge as she climbed the stairs, got him settled, and finally left his room.

She breathed a sigh of relief and mentally went through a list of what all she should try to get done before he was awake again. It was already nearly two in the afternoon. Bonnie got the kitchen cleaned up, picked up the living room, and went back upstairs. She wanted to check on Gunner but stopped at the large window.

The sky had darkened with lightning flashing in the distance. It was hard to tell which direction the thunderstorm was heading.

The front door opened and closed again. "Bonnie?"

"Upstairs." She called loud enough to let Jace know without waking up Gunner.

He appeared at the top of the landing. "How's Gunner? I had a few minutes and thought I would stop by and check on him."

Bonnie smiled. "He's asleep and has been for about two hours now. Poor guy was miserable all morning." She tilted her head toward the window and turned back to look outside. "It sure is pouring back there."

Even the clouds appeared to be falling out of the sky and streaking toward the ground.

Footsteps told her Jace was coming closer. He must have stopped just behind her because she could smell the combination of leather and sunshine.

Jace spoke, and the close proximity of his voice confirmed his location. "I checked a while ago, and the storm should miss us. We might get a little rain, but nothing too major."

Bonnie nodded. "That's good." She tried to think of something else to say, but every cell in her body was attuned to Jace. It'd be easier if he moved away and gave her a little space to focus. "I'm just glad we don't get tornadoes here in Clearwater. Or at least they are so few and far between, we may as well not get them at all."

"Me, too. Although I rather like the thunderstorms. There's something about the natural power of them that demands respect."

Bonnie was about to comment when her phone rang. She

saw Wyatt's name and answered quickly, hoping it wouldn't wake Gunner. "Hey, big brother. Are you getting any rain at the stables?"

The line was silent until her brother made a sound like he was clearing his throat. "Hey, Bon. Chrissy needs me, but we could use your prayers. We lost the baby." The last word came out broken. "There was no heartbeat at our appointment."

"Oh, Wyatt." Tears clogged her throat as she tried to wrap her brain around the horrible news. "I'm sorry. I can't even imagine…is there anything I can do?"

"Not now. Just pray. I'll reach out in the next day or so."

"Okay. I love you both."

Wyatt's voice was so low, it was hard to hear. "I love you too." The call ended then.

Woodenly, Bonnie slipped the phone into her back pocket and took in a slow breath, willing herself to keep her emotions in check until Jace headed back out again.

She thought about Wyatt and Chrissy and the loss of her sweet baby niece or nephew and a sob caught in her throat.

JACE STOOD BEHIND BONNIE AS SHE ENDED HER PHONE CALL. Her shoulders drooped and moments later, her chin followed. He'd heard part of the conversation, and it was clear something terrible had happened. "Bonnie?"

She covered her face with her hands as her shoulders shook silently.

Jace stepped around her and gently pulled her into his arms. She resisted for only a moment before letting herself lean into his chest.

He held her close as she cried, breathed in the fresh scent

of her hair, and wished he could do something—anything—to ease her grief.

"The baby?"

Bonnie nodded.

"I'm sorry," Jace whispered. To lose a child, no matter what stage of development, would be devastating. He thought of Gunner asleep in the other room, and his throat ached with emotion. "I'll be praying for your brother and his wife."

"I appreciate it." She sniffed and accepted the handkerchief he handed to her. "They desperately wanted that baby. I wish I understood why things like this happen."

Jace wished he could offer some kind of wisdom to help, but the truth was, he had no idea either. "Sometimes I think it would be good to understand. And other times, I'm not sure that it would make the loss any easier."

Bonnie folded the handkerchief twice in her hand and nodded nervously. "I usually make it my policy not to cry in front of my employer. I'm sure I look like a complete mess right now."

There were a lot of things Jace could've said, but the only thing that came to his mind spilled right out of his mouth. "You have nothing to worry about. You look beautiful, Bonnie. You always do."

Judging by the surprise in her eyes, he wasn't sure which of them was more shocked by his words. He'd thought she was beautiful since the first day he met her. But to tell her out loud? He'd never considered doing such a thing before.

Her brown eyes pulled him in. He reached up and gently touched her cheek with the pad of one thumb. She drew in a sharp breath. Her cheeks turned pink, but she never pulled her gaze from his. Instinct drew him closer until their lips were a breath apart.

Gunner started to cry, the sound causing concern for his son to war with his intense disappointment that the moment was broken. All of that punctuated by the realization of what he'd nearly done.

Bonnie moved to get Gunner, and Jace put a hand on her arm to stop her. "It's okay, I'll get him. We should check his temperature again. Do you want to find the thermometer?"

"Of course." She glanced down where his hand still rested on her arm. "Jace…"

Her tone held every cautionary thought that was already screaming in his own mind. "I know."

Here she'd just received bad news, and he would've kissed her had Gunner not started crying.

So stupid.

Gunner was already out of bed and trying to open his bedroom door when Jace got there. He picked up his son and frowned at the heat emanating from his little body. "Hey, buddy. I came to check on you. Did you have a good nap?"

They found Bonnie again at the bottom of the stairs. She ran the temporal thermometer across his forehead and held the reading up for Jace to see.

"One hundred point six," he read aloud. "It could be worse. Hopefully whatever this is will be short-lived." Jace patted Gunner on the back. His son wiggled to get down and immediately ran to his riding car. "I wish I were that active when I'm sick."

Bonnie chuckled. "I hear you."

There was some silence as they both tried not to look at each other. Jace finally broke it. "If you need time off to help your brother, please just let me know."

She shook her head. "He said he needs some space. He'll let me know when he's ready." Her voice was quiet. "I'll probably send flowers. I wish I could do more." She gave a defeated shrug. "Thank you, though."

"Okay. Well, I'd better get back to work. I'll see you tonight. Don't hesitate to call if you need anything." It was something he said most days before he left the house. Today, though, it was different. Jace wanted Bonnie to share her day with him.

Their near kiss came to mind, and Jace wasn't sure which was worse: That he'd nearly kissed the nanny, or that he was having a difficult time not wishing he'd succeeded.

Chapter Thirteen

Bonnie wasn't sure who was avoiding whom more. All she knew was that she saw Jace briefly when she went to the main house to care for Gunner. Jace was ready to go, gave his son a hug, and wished them a good day.

In the evening, it was Bonnie's turn to be ready to leave as soon as Jace or Noel walked in the door. When it was Noel, Bonnie enjoyed visiting with her for a few minutes first.

Noel had asked several times last week if Bonnie would join them for dinner. Bonnie always turned down the invitation, though guilt was beginning to build when it came to Noel. Honestly, she was pretty sure she and Noel could be friends if given the opportunity.

It was better to go back to a situation like they had before the move to the ranch. One where she and Jace only talked about Gunner and anything related to him. Not one where he told her all about his family. Or where she cried on his shoulder.

Ugh, why did she have to cry in front of him like that? It'd been instinctual to put his arms around her, which only made it worse.

She swore he was about to kiss her, too, if Gunner hadn't started to cry. And if Jace had? Yep, she was pretty sure she would've kissed him back.

And now things were awkward.

Avoiding each other probably was the best thing they could be doing right now.

Except for one small problem: She missed him. She'd started getting used to these glimpses into who he really was. A man who had her heart twisted up in all kinds of knots.

Taking the weekend to decompress helped some. She'd spent the time making meals for Wyatt and Chrissy. She saw them briefly on Sunday when she dropped them off after church. The anguish on their faces broke her heart.

If only she could do more. But only time would help. That and a lot of prayer.

After having way too much time to herself over the weekend, Monday was a welcome arrival. It was beautiful outside—and she needed the distraction—so she set out on a short walk.

She followed the fence line away from the house along the property in back. It was almost chilly this morning, and she crossed her arms in front of her to keep herself warm. Once she'd reached the back of the property, she spotted the barn. If she had more time, she'd consider walking over there to see if she could spot any of the new lambs that Jace had been talking about.

A voice to her left made her jump. She whirled around to find one of the guys that worked on the ranch watching her. "Can I help you find something?"

She couldn't remember his name. "I'm sorry, you're…"

"Elvin. Ma'am." He tilted his head just a little. "Is there something you need?"

She shook her head. "I just thought I'd take a walk before I started work. It's a lovely morning, isn't it?"

He gave her a barely-perceptible nod. He definitely wasn't the chatty type.

"I guess I'd better be getting back. Have a good day, Elvin."

"You, too." He disappeared into the trees leaving Bonnie alone again. No longer in the mood for a walk, she headed back to the house.

As expected, Jace was waiting, his boots on, and looking like he was ready to bolt. "Good morning," he greeted.

"Good morning. How's Gunner doing?"

"He acted normal all weekend. And even better, neither Noel or I have gotten sick. I trust you managed to avoid catching it as well?"

"I did." She slipped her hands, which were picking at the hem of her shirt, into the pockets of her jeans. Sheesh, this was one of the most formal conversations they'd had in a while. "The weather is beautiful outside today. Hopefully it'll make your job easier."

"I'm sure it will." Gunner ran in and Jace picked him up and hugged him close. "You be good for Miss Bonnie today. I love you, buddy." Jace set him down on the ground and turned to Bonnie. "Call if you need anything."

"Will do." She waved goodbye and watched until he closed the door behind him. Only then did she relax a little and focus on her young charge. "What should we do today?"

JACE HATED HOW HIS CONVERSATIONS WITH BONNIE WERE much shorter now. Like they used to be before they'd all moved to the ranch. Before she'd started to relax around him because he'd lowered his guard and let her in.

He frowned.

Monday had been a little awkward, and he'd hoped it

would get better as the week progressed. Now it was Thursday, and he was beginning to hate the way he'd handled things. Maybe he should've just kissed her anyway. Or at least talked to her about it. The end result couldn't have been much weirder. Instead, they'd ignored the giant elephant in the room, and it'd only managed to get bigger.

At least that's the way it seemed to him.

One thing was certain: it'd served as enough of a distraction that he'd almost forgotten about the damaged fence. Until now.

Jace stood with Cabe and surveyed the section of fencing that had been knocked down in a completely different field. Deep ruts in the ground revealed more than one vehicle had gone through into the field.

That wasn't the worst of it, though.

Every last sheep in that field was gone. Thankfully, it was a small fraction of the herd. However, this field contained the ewes who recently gave birth along with their lambs.

Livestock that was vital to keep the ranch going.

Jace snatched the hat off his head and whacked it hard against a nearby fence post.

"What are we going to do now, Cabe?"

The older man released a heavy sigh. "Exactly what your grandfather would do. We'll pick ourselves up by the bootstraps and keep on keeping on. We've got a number of ewes about to birth. There's a good buffer built into the ranch's finances to help weather a rough year or two."

Jace scratched his head. "I'm worried that we've got someone getting onto the property and messing around at night. If they got away with stealing last night, what's to say they won't try it again?" He didn't like the idea of someone stealing from him. But he disliked the thought of someone sneaking around the ranch at night with Gunner, Noel, and Bonnie there even more.

"I'll report it to the police. Let's fix this fencing, and we'll go from there. We need to move the flock to the fields closest to the houses or barn."

"Agreed. Let's get to it."

It was truly a grueling day. By the time Jace headed home, he was tired, hungry, and concerned. Noel's car was parked in front. He'd been gone longer than he realized.

When he entered the house, he found Bonnie and Noel in the kitchen, chatting like old friends. Both women were cheerful until they noticed him, and the smiles faltered.

"What happened?" Noel asked.

"All done!" Gunner announced, holding up hands covered with flour.

"You did a great job." Bonnie picked him up and took him to the sink where they worked on washing his hands. She glanced back at Jace, though, unease on her face.

Jace told them about the fencing and the stolen sheep. "I can't even think about how much money we lost today." He'd have to work it all out in the books soon, but not right now.

Now he had to figure out what they could do to make sure this didn't happen again. "I'm sorry I'm late. We moved the herds closer to the house and barn to keep a better eye on them."

"It's too bad we can't put surveillance cameras up along the fence line," Noel said with a frown. "Except it would cost a small fortune."

Bonnie set Gunner down. "Is there any indication that this was the same set of people who tore down the panels before?"

"We have no way of knowing." Which truly frustrated Jace. "I filed a report, the police came down and took our statements and a bunch of pictures. No other reports of stolen animals or damaged property in the area. I'm hoping the two weren't connected and this is the end of it all, but..." Yeah, he just couldn't quite convince himself of that. This made three separate issues on the ranch. He didn't believe in coincidences.

Noel hopped up to sit on the countertop. "You don't suppose our parents might have hired someone to mess things up for us?"

The thought had crossed his mind. What if Noel was right? The sad thing was, he knew they were capable of it. But was there enough motive? The ranch belonged to him and Noel. If they sold it, they'd split the money two ways. None of it would go to their parents. "I seriously doubt it. For one, what would they gain?" Originally, he'd assumed it was all about money with them. What if it was as much of a control thing instead?

Their parents were desperate, but surely not to the point of ruining their children's goals just out of spite.

Jace wished he felt more confident about that. He watched as Bonnie slid something into the oven and then went to stir a pot on the stove. She looked like she belonged in his kitchen, something that had him desperately shoving such thoughts into the back of his mind.

Bonnie wiped her hands on a towel. "The cornbread should be done in about twelve minutes. There's stew in the pot there for you all. I'll head back home and let you guys relax for a while." She knelt down and held her arms out to Gunner. "See you tomorrow."

Jace watched as she gathered his son into her arms and kissed him on the head.

Noel hopped off the counter and onto her feet. "I wish you'd stay and have dinner with us, Bonnie." She looked at Jace as if she expected him to jump in. "You go to all of this effort here and then what do you eat when you get home?"

Poor Bonnie looked from Noel to Jace and back again. "You guys need your space. I'm okay with that—I always have been." She stood, one hand resting on Gunner's shoulder.

Jace wanted to argue with her, but it was clear she needed an escape. He offered a smile. "I'll walk you to the apartment door."

Bonnie stood. "You don't need to do that." She waved at Noel and told her goodbye before retrieving her bag in the living room.

Jace didn't care that it wasn't a long walk. He wouldn't let Noel walk alone right now, either. "Just humor me on walking you to your place. I'd do it for anyone here on the ranch, trust me."

"So you walked Cabe back to the barn then?" She kept a serious face, although humor twinkled in her eyes.

"Okay, almost anyone." Jace grinned. "Come on." He went to the front door and opened it for her. Once she went through ahead of him, they walked side-by-side around the house to the large garage. Jace was satisfied to note the main door was still locked. "See? That wasn't so hard." He had every intention of telling her goodbye now, except it was the first time he'd talked to her in days outside of the general hello and goodbyes they exchanged. "You've been avoiding me."

Bonnie's eyes widened. But to her credit, she didn't waver. "Maybe. I'm not the only one who's playing the avoidance game, though."

"True." Jace ought to wish her good night and walk away now. His feet refused to listen. "For the record, I kind of got used to seeing you more before. I've missed that." Some of his favorite memories of the last few weeks there at the ranch were times spent with Bonnie. Suddenly, he needed to know whether she felt the same way.

Just when he thought she was going to turn around and go

inside, she shifted her feet and wrapped a section of hair around one finger. "Yeah. Me, too."

Jace went out on a limb. "Look, I know I'm the one who put all of these strict boundaries in place from the beginning. But I've enjoyed getting to know you more, and I'd like it if we could be friends."

"I'm not sure that's a good idea." Bonnie appeared doubtful as she tugged on the hem of her sleeve. A completely adorable little quirk of hers.

"I just know I could always use more friends. Couldn't you?"

She nodded slowly as though weighing the pros and cons of the possibility. "Yeah, I could, too."

Jace had to fight to keep from smiling in triumph. "Awesome. Friends, then?" He held a hand out. When she slipped her petite hand into his, he gave it a solid shake and let go. "As my first act as an official friend, I'd like to ask you how your brother is doing. And are you doing okay after everything?"

Sadness clouded Bonnie's features, but she seemed to appreciate the question. "They are struggling. It hasn't been easy, but they have a lot of support. I've been worried about them. Wyatt and Chrissy are such great friends, though. They've really been there for each other."

Jace was glad to hear that. He knew that a loss of any kind could put distance between a married couple. He'd seen it happen with friends and even some more distant relatives. He knew, without a doubt, that it would have been a struggle for him and Samantha. The kind of relationship Wyatt and Chrissy had sounded like the kind he hoped to have one day for himself.

"I'm glad they are doing okay, though I'm sorry they are going through this at all. It's good you can be there for them."

"Thanks, I appreciate it." Bonnie looked thoughtful. "And

as my first act as an official friend, I'd like to invite you, Noel, and Gunner to visit my church one of these Sundays. I have some family members that attend. Thankfully, none of the annoying ones." She chuckled, but there was an underlying hint of nervousness there. "No pressure, just wanted to extend the invitation."

Jace hadn't gone to church regularly in a while. He'd just been thinking about how that should change, especially now that Gunner was getting a little older. Going with Bonnie would be a bonus. "I'd like that, and I'm sure Noel would, too. Thank you."

He made a mental note as she told him the church's name and time.

She tipped her head toward the main house. "You'd better get back before Noel and Gunner eat without you."

"Yeah, I probably should." He grinned at her. "Have a good night, Bonnie."

"You, too. Thanks for walking me home."

Jace tipped his invisible hat. He forced himself to turn away from the beautiful woman who he was quickly falling in love with, despite his best efforts to avoid exactly that.

Chapter Fourteen

Bonnie lost track of how many times she glanced at the door leading into the church's worship hall. She tried to keep it subtle, but this time, Wyatt nudged her shoulder. "If you're looking for Chrissy, Gran is with her and they said they'd be back in a few minutes."

"Yeah. I mean, no, that's not who..." She stopped and sighed. "I invited Jace, Noel, and Gunner to come to church."

Wyatt kept his face neutral, though there was no missing the interest in his eyes. "That was a good move, Bon." He put an arm around her shoulder. "Are things still weird between the two of you?"

"Maybe not as weird. But yeah." Bonnie shrugged. "It shouldn't be this hard."

"You know what Gran would say."

Together, they repeated, "If it's worth it, then it's worth doing something about it."

A voice spoke up from behind them. "I'm glad to hear that my words of wisdom aren't lost on the younger generation." Gran chuckled as she joined them, shortly followed by Chrissy.

Wyatt reached for his wife's hand and drew her to his

side.

Bonnie watched them for several moments. He'd been so sweet to Chrissy since their miscarriage nearly two weeks ago. And Chrissy had leaned into him for strength. The two of them were an inspiration. Bonnie was just glad to see that at least a little of the sorrow in her sister-in-law's eyes was easing.

She stepped around Wyatt to give Chrissy a hug. "You doing okay?"

Chrissy nodded. "A little better every day."

Bonnie went to stand in front of her chair and then turned to hug Gran, too, who took the seat next to hers. "Hi, Gran. And for the record? I consider your wisdom worth more than gold. At least most of it." She gave her grandmother a wink.

Gran patted her hand with a loving smile.

Bonnie looked around the church and soaked in the contentment and love that always filled the building. It wasn't just the four walls, though. It was the people that filled it. She'd been coming here with Gran since she was young, and it would always be another home for her.

The countdown on the projector screen showed less than five minutes until worship would begin.

Bonnie was tempted to look at the door again but forced herself to focus on the screen in front of her. Staring at the door certainly wasn't going to make Jace appear. And even if he did visit their church, it didn't mean anything anyway.

She'd just about convinced herself of that when a deep voice spoke from behind her, immediately sending goose-bumps racing across her skin.

"Good morning, Bonnie."

What was it about his voice that had her pulse dancing? She took a slow breath in as she schooled her response and then turned to find Jace and Noel in the row right behind her. "Good morning." She noted the absence of a particularly active little boy. "Did someone help you find Gunner's class?"

Jace nodded. "As soon as Gunner saw the bin of toys, he never looked back."

Noel reached over and gave Bonnie a hug. "Everyone here has been so welcoming. Thank you for inviting us."

"You're welcome. I'm glad you're here." Bonnie realized that their interactions had snagged the attention of her family. She barely had a chance to make the introductions before the church's worship team began to play music. Moments later, the room filled with song as the lyrics appeared on the screen at the front of the room.

It took nearly everything Bonnie had in her to focus on worship and then the message instead of the man who was sitting directly behind her.

When she'd invited him to join her at church, she had no idea whether he would accept or not. Now that he had, she wondered whether it was simply because he was looking for a church home himself. Was it horrible that a big part of her secretly hoped there was more to it than that?

She swallowed a groan and tried to focus on the announcements the associate pastor was sharing. After a final prayer, the congregation was dismissed. Bonnie tucked her Bible under one arm and retrieved her bag from beneath her chair.

The aisles were full as people maneuvered their way to the back of the church. As had become their habit, they waited with Gran until the aisle cleared and it was easier for her to walk.

Gran turned in her seat to address Jace and Noel. "It's good to finally meet you both. I've heard a lot about you."

Jace chuckled. "All good, I hope."

"It depends on who I heard it from." Gran gave him a mischievous wink while reaching over to pat Jace's hand.

"But don't you worry, comments have been positive from those who count."

Bonnie's cheeks grew hot, and she wished she could hide her face right now. What must Jace be thinking? That she went around talking about him all the time to Gran?

She risked a peek at him to find him watching her, amusement mixed with curiosity on his face, but there was nothing but warmth in his eyes.

Gran ran a hand over the skirt of her dress. "My wonderful grandkids here eat lunch with me every Sunday after church. We'd love it if you'd join us. We're just going to the café down the street." As if that settled everything, she put the strap of her purse over her shoulder and headed for the aisle.

Jace and Noel glanced at each other before he said, "We don't want to intrude."

"You wouldn't be," Wyatt assured him while Chrissy nodded, her arm through her husband's. "We're going to Clearwater Café. We can meet you there after you get Gunner from his class."

Bonnie worried they would feel pressured. "If you had other plans, you aren't obligated to come. Gran makes friends everywhere, and she's one of the most outspoken people I know." She was giving Jace an out, but her heart held onto hope that he was going to join them for lunch anyway.

Jace moved as though he thought about reaching out to Bonnie. Instead, he tucked his hands into the pockets of his jeans. "I don't want you to be uncomfortable. Are you sure you wouldn't mind if we ate lunch with you all?"

Noel followed the conversation back and forth, her head moving to face the person speaking. It would've been funny if Bonnie hadn't been nervous. "I'd like you all to come."

There. She said it. Now it was completely up to him.

"In that case, it sounds like fun. I'll go get Gunner, and

we'll meet you there." With that, Jace strode past and to the back of the room.

Noel didn't say a word, but she did give Bonnie a knowing look before following her brother.

When the Echolls siblings were gone, Wyatt moved to put an arm around Chrissy and smiled at Bonnie. "I'd say your plan is working."

Chrissy was all but rubbing her hands together in excitement.

Bonnie wanted to object but smiled instead. "It wasn't a plan, simply an invitation. You two are jumping to conclusions. This doesn't mean anything."

"Sure it does." Wyatt put his other arm around Bonnie. "The man would be dumb and blind if he didn't accept your invitation or Gran's." He raised his brows. "Now we'll see if he's worthy of my little sister."

Bonnie jabbed him in the ribs with her elbow, but his comment had her smiling. "Don't scare him away, Wyatt."

"I promise nothing." He hugged both women close. "Come on, I'm starving."

*

IT ALWAYS AMAZED JACE HOW MUCH WORK IT TOOK TO KEEP a two-year-old entertained at a restaurant. At least the Clearwater Café had bread and honey butter on the tables to enjoy while they waited for their meals. Thankfully, Gunner was a big fan of bread.

Jace glanced across the long table they were all sitting at and let his gaze rest on Bonnie. She swept some hair out of her eyes and then spread a thick layer of honey butter on a slice of homemade bread.

One of these days, he'd like to take her out for a meal. Just the two of them. What would she say if he asked her?

He tried to focus on the conversation around him as everyone else visited. Wyatt was talking about Joyful Hope Stables. Jace remembered a time last year when Bonnie's car quit working, and Wyatt dropped her off at Jace's house for work. They'd met briefly as Jace headed out the door. He mentally cringed at how much he worked back then.

Jace gave Gunner another piece of bread then asked, "Joyful Hope sounds amazing. Are the patients that go there referred from any particular medical facility, or do people make their own arrangements?"

"Both." Wyatt wiped his hands off on a napkin. "Most of the kids in our hippotherapy sessions are from the rehabilitation center where they receive physical therapy, occupational therapy, or both. One of Chrissy's friends, Raven, works there and learned about the stables. She thought a lot of the kids would benefit from it." He smiled, and it was clear he was proud of what they did. "We probably have as many senior citizens as we do kids, though. It just depends on the day of the week."

Gran, as everyone seemed to call her, pointed a finger at Wyatt. "Walking away from the Tabor fortune was the best thing you could've ever done."

"I couldn't agree more," Wyatt affirmed.

Jace smiled. "Would it be okay to drop by sometime? I'd enjoy seeing the place after hearing so much about it."

Wyatt gave a subtle nod. "You'd be welcome anytime."

But it was the glitter of approval in Bonnie's eyes that mattered the most to Jace. "Wyatt and Chrissy have already had to expand once since opening a year ago. The stables are growing by leaps and bounds."

Wyatt reached for his wife's hand. "A lot of people worked hard to make this a reality. Our large volunteer base is what keeps things running the way they do."

Bonnie shook her head as she addressed Jace. "He's way

too modest. He and Chrissy are the heart behind Joyful Hope Stables, and don't let him convince you otherwise."

Her loyalty and encouragement had Wyatt smiling at her, but it also filled Jace with pride. He knew how important it was to have Noel's support and to know Bonnie was the kind of woman who helped her brother was just one of the many reasons why he'd fallen in love with her.

The realization struck him as surely as a blow. He was completely, head over heels, in love. And it wasn't a recent thing, either.

Jace had loved Bonnie for months. Maybe longer. But he hadn't allowed himself to even consider the possibility.

Until now.

Now, he could picture building a life with this woman by his side. He imagined raising Gunner together.

God, is this real? I know she adores Gunner like a mom would, but could she love me as I love her?

His heart soared, and he had to force himself to focus on the conversation shifting around him and the food that was being placed on the table. Bonnie had been hesitant to be friends with him; if he told her how he felt now, he was afraid she might pull back.

As much as he'd love to talk to her tonight, he needed to give it some time. The last thing he wanted to do was make a mess out of something that had potential.

For now, he enjoyed lunch and watching Bonnie with her family. She was relaxed, and at one point, laughed at something Wyatt said until she had tears in her eyes. He wanted to laugh with her like that one day.

His thoughts briefly switched to Samantha. For the first time, there was no guilt there. No comparison. It was simply an acknowledgment that things were different, and that was okay.

It was okay to love Bonnie.

Chapter Fifteen

✦✦✦

It was a whole lot easier to be friends with Jace than it was to avoid him. Bonnie wasn't sure which had been harder: Ignoring how she felt about Jace or barely talking to him for a while. When Noel had commented about Jace caring for her, it'd given Bonnie some hope. Until Jace said he wanted to be friends. The idea of not being more than friends resulted in stabs of disappointment that she had to fight to ignore.

Until he'd accepted her invitation to church. Not only that, but he'd joined them for lunch, too. It'd been surreal to have the two biggest parts of her life—which she'd kept completely separate before—essentially in a room interacting together.

It'd been wonderful.

But where did that leave her and Jace?

Speaking of her handsome employer, it was Monday, and he was running a little late today getting home, and so was Noel. It was frustrating because no matter what she told herself about them being friends, she still couldn't wait to see him when he got home.

She played with Gunner and tried to keep the little boy

busy. Dinner was in the slow cooker, and honestly, the day had dragged by.

As though it had been orchestrated, the front door opened to admit both Noel and Jace. Noel waved her hands around, her voice raised.

"The next time she bothers me at work with one of her 'talks,' things are going to get downright uncivilized."

Bonnie tried not to chuckle since she could hardly picture Noel as being anything but civil to anyone. Instead, she focused on the tower of blocks she and Gunner were building and tried not to listen in on their conversation. It was impossible.

Jace closed the door harder than necessary. "You need to tell the people up front that they shouldn't allow Mother through without your approval first. She assumes everyone will rearrange their lives for her, and when they don't, she manipulates things in her favor."

"I'd like to think we proved she doesn't have control over us by taking over the ranch." Noel sank to the couch near Bonnie with a satisfied smile on her face. "I sure don't lose sleep over it."

"Me either," Jace agreed. "Speaking of the ranch, I need to eat fast and get back out to the barn. I may be out there most of the night."

That had Bonnie's attention. She sat upright and focused on Jace. "What's going on?"

"We're stretched thin. Cabe had to go out of town for a couple of days. Brady and Elvin are taking shifts patrolling the fence line and keeping an eye on the herds. Meanwhile, we have a ewe that's in labor with twins and having some difficulty. I'm going to stay in the barn and keep an eye on her. Make sure we get the lambs here safely. After having so many stolen, we can't afford to lose either of them."

Noel nodded. "I've got Gunner tonight. No worries. I hope the little ones make it okay."

Bonnie did, too. "I'd be happy to help if you need me."

Immediately, Jace shook his head. "I couldn't ask you to do that. Who knows how long we'll be out there?"

"You're not asking, I'm volunteering." Bonnie stood. "I've wanted to learn more about the sheep anyway. This sounds like a great opportunity."

Jace and Noel exchanged a look Bonnie couldn't quite decipher before Jace offered her a smile. "If you're sure."

Bonnie grinned. "Absolutely. I'll go home, get a few things together, and be ready to go. What time should I meet you here?"

Jace glanced at his watch, gave her a time, and Bonnie left. She jogged around the house, ate something quick, changed clothes, and packed a few snacks and a couple bottles of water in her bag before going back to the main house. Jace was already waiting for her out on the swing. He stood when she came into view.

"You ready?"

"I think so."

"This way, then." Jace led the way to his truck where he opened the passenger door for her. "The ewe we're going to be keeping an eye on tonight was one of Grandpa's favorites. She has twins as often as not, and this pregnancy is no exception." He closed the door and went around to the driver's side. "She's experienced, and she knows what to do, but I'm afraid the first lamb's positioning is off. We're going to watch her closely, and if she shows any signs of distress, I'll manually turn the lamb and help guide it out."

Bonnie had only seen births on television but had always found it fascinating. "You know how to do that?"

"I helped Grandpa more than once, but it's been a while."

"Are you nervous?" Bonnie would be. She was a little now just going in to help.

He gave her a crooked smile as he started the truck. "Yep. Not going to lie, I wish Cabe were here."

The raw honesty in his eyes had Bonnie's heart sighing. The guy had no idea how appealing he was. That quality drew her in more.

They arrived at the barn and hurried inside. Bonnie instantly sympathized with the ewe as she watched the animal pace back and forth in a stall, her sides bulging, and her sweet eyes relaying her discomfort.

"You poor thing," Bonnie crooned as Jace climbed into the stall and felt along her sides. Bonnie wanted to go into the stall as well, but wasn't sure she would be welcome. She didn't want to crowd the poor thing. "What's her name?"

Jace gave the ewe a satisfied pat on the rump and backed up to the railing near Bonnie. "Molly. She's one of the calmest sheep I've ever met."

Poor Molly laid down on the ground as contractions began. She let her head rest on her front legs and let out little grunts. "How long does this process take?"

"It completely depends, but once the lamb's hooves emerge, it's usually an hour or less until birth." He tipped his head toward the animal. "But Molly here is quite experienced, and usually doesn't have as long of a labor as she's having. I'm going to get a few supplies so we're prepared." He returned momentarily with a couple of wooden stools that he set just inside the stall. "Here, you can sit in there to wait and watch."

"Are you sure I won't be bothering her?" The last thing Bonnie wanted to do was stress the poor mama-to-be out.

"I'm sure." He opened the small gate and let her in. "I'll be right back."

Bonnie claimed one of the stools and kept an eye on

Molly, half expecting the sheep to object to her presence. Instead, the poor thing struggled to her feet where she took several steps and turned, almost as if she were pacing. A few minutes later, she paused and grunted multiple times, her sides heaving with each one.

When Jace returned, Bonnie released a silent sigh of relief. "The poor thing looks miserable." She watched as he arranged several things on the ground near the stools, including some thin rope and blankets. He left again. This time, it only took a few minutes to return. He set down a pail of water.

Jace nodded, his eyes sympathetic as he watched Molly. "Yes, she does. But at least things are finally starting to happen." He pointed at Molly's tail. "There we go. Those are the lamb's front hooves."

Bonnie leaned forward to catch a glimpse. The moment she saw the tiny hooves making their entrance, her heart soared. She couldn't wait to see what one of the little lambs looked like.

Molly stumbled to her feet and paced, grunting with the effort. When contractions started again, she laid back down.

"I remember the first time Grandpa took me with him to observe a birth," Jace said, his voice wistful. "I was probably seven or eight. I didn't do much—just sat and watched. But there's something about the miracle of life that amazes me every time." His voice caught.

Bonnie turned her head to look at him. She swallowed back the sadness when she saw the depth of emotion in his eyes. Of course, it would be hard for him to do this for the first time without his grandpa. "I'm sorry, Jace. I shouldn't have come out here. If you'd rather I go back to the house, please let me know."

He blinked at her for a moment and smiled. "No, I'm glad you're here. I'm sometimes surprised at what makes me miss

Grandpa. I'm a little sad now, but I hope every time I come out here during a lambing, it reminds me of him."

"It's good you have that, Jace."

They watched Molly for some time, and Jace explained how the birthing process would go. But unlike his explanation, the hooves never descended past a certain point. When Molly's head rolled to the side and her sounds of effort intensified, Jace stood.

"We should be seeing the lamb's nose by now. It should be lying over its knees. If the head is back, it's no wonder the poor girl is having trouble." He rolled his sleeves up and began to wash his hands in the pail of water, using a bottle of soap in the process. "I'm going to check the presentation. If we're right, Molly's going to need some help."

Once his hands were clean, he grabbed a coil of thin rope and slowly approached Molly. Bonnie watched as he ran a hand down her side.

"Hey, girl," he said softly. "You're doing an amazing job, but this baby just doesn't want to cooperate, does it?"

Bonnie could've sworn the ewe gave him a look of relief.

Jace talked Bonnie through everything as he checked the lamb's position. "Yeah, its head is back." He made a noose with the rope. "I'm going to put this over the forelimbs, guide the head around, and slip the rope over its head to help bring the lamb down into position."

Molly complained as he worked. "It's okay, sweet girl," Jace reassured her. "You're doing a great job as always."

Bonnie folded her hands together and watched as, with some effort, Jace accomplished his task. When the lamb's nose and face became visible along with the legs, she realized what he meant and why he could tell something had been wrong.

"Alright." Jace softly patted Molly's side. "We'll wait for

another round of contractions, and then I'll help you out a little."

It didn't take long for the contractions to begin again. Jace gently pulled on the rope that was around the lamb. Molly bleated with effort as the lamb finally slid onto the ground.

"There we are," Jace announced proudly. "Looks like we've got a baby boy here. Good job, Molly. Bonnie, would you bring me a blanket, please?"

Glad she could finally help in some way, she snatched the top blanket and went forward to hand it to him.

The lamb was mostly still, and Bonnie held her breath hoping it was going to be okay.

Jace used the blanket to wipe the lamb's mouth and face off. "There we go. We need to make sure his nose and mouth are clear so he can breathe. Then we need to help clear his airway a little." He picked up the lamb by the back legs and held it upside down for several minutes before lowering him back to the ground.

The lamb's sides moved as he breathed, and Molly stretched her neck to reach her baby. She began to lick his ears.

Bonnie grinned. "He's so tiny." His entire body was white except for the black on his head. "Good job, Molly. Look at you, you're such a good mama."

As though encouraged by Bonnie's words, Molly continued to clean her lamb until contractions began again.

"Hopefully the second lamb will be easier for her." Jace nodded toward the stack of blankets. "Grab another and you can help me dry this little guy off since Molly's going to be busy for a few minutes."

Together, they worked to gently clean the lamb until he was nearly dry. Jace wrapped him in a clean towel and held him out to Bonnie. "Why don't you hold the lamb and keep him warm while we wait for the other baby?"

He immediately placed the lamb in her arms, and Bonnie was surprised by how light he was. She took several steps back before settling on the hay with the little guy in her arms. She gently ran a finger over his long ear.

When she glanced up again, she found Jace watching her, a tender expression on his face. "You're a natural."

He was probably only being kind, but his words warmed her. "Thank you for letting me be a part of this."

"I'm glad you wanted to be."

Thankfully, Jace was right, and poor Molly didn't have nearly as hard of a time delivering the second lamb. The nose presented itself along with the hooves. In a fraction of the time, the little one made its appearance.

"And we have a girl," Jace announced as he cleaned off the lamb's face. He smiled at the ewe. "You did it, Molly." He motioned to Bonnie. "Bring yours over and put him down by Molly. She'll focus on him while we get this one all cleaned up."

The moment Bonnie placed the baby on the hay next to Molly, the ewe immediately took over care. Molly got to her feet, and Bonnie watched in amazement as the baby tried to do the same and stumbled on spindly legs to find a nipple and nurse. Bonnie had to resist the urge to squeal at how cute it all was.

Jace finished drying off the ewe lamb and released it near her mama. Then he moved to stand next to Bonnie as they watched the twins eat their first meal.

"They'll be okay now?"

He nodded. "Molly's only ever lost one lamb, and it was stillborn. These two should be fine." He held his hands out in front of him and wrinkled his nose. "I need a serious hand scrubbing."

She thought about him turning the lamb and laughed. "Yeah, I'll bet you do."

He pointed to the pail of water. "You can use that and the soap there if you'd like. I'm going to go scrub in the bathroom here in the barn, and I'll be back shortly."

Bonnie washed her hands and dried them on a clean towel. A yawn caught her by surprise as she set the towel down and glanced at her watch. It was after one in the morning. She'd had no idea so much time passed since they got here.

Suddenly tired, she sat on the hay on the ground, her back against the wooden slats of the barn stall.

She thought about how easily Jace had taken control of the situation with Molly. Talking to him in the truck, he'd said he was nervous. He shouldn't have been, though. It was clear running the ranch was exactly what he was meant to do.

The man was an amazing dad, great with animals, and commanded situations with ease. Was it truly that far of a stretch to understand why her own heart belonged to him as well?

JACE FINISHED CLEANING UP. WHEN HE RETURNED TO Molly's stall, he found Bonnie sitting on the ground, her arms resting on her knees, and a look of happy exhaustion on her face.

She'd been such a trooper through the whole ordeal, and a big help as well. He'd never doubted her ability to assist out here. They'd worked seamlessly together, and Jace enjoyed every minute of it.

They hadn't even argued about anything this evening, either. He chuckled to himself.

Molly and her lambs were doing wonderfully. It should mean he and Bonnie were clear to head back home. Or rather, their respective homes. Jace yawned. Maybe he could catch a couple hours of sleep before it was time to get back to work.

He walked over and crouched down next to Bonnie. "Hey, you awake?" A hand on her shoulder brought her eyes to his face.

"I'm awake—but barely. Both of the lambs are nursing. They seem to be doing well, don't they?"

"They do. They'll be safe and warm in here. We should go back and get some sleep." He stood and reached a hand down toward her. Once she placed her smaller hand in his, he helped her stand.

"That sounds good. Seven-thirty will come early today."

"Yes, it will. I figured I might start work late. You can wait and come in at nine. See if you can sleep in a little."

Bonnie raised an eyebrow. She tipped her head to one side looking at his ear and then the other before getting up on her toes.

"What are you doing?" he asked, trying not to laugh at her odd behavior.

"I'm looking for alien antennae or anything else suggesting you've been taken over. I've never known you to go in to work late."

She laughed then, and he joined her, although there was a part of him that was saddened by the fact that she clearly saw him as a workaholic. Of course, that's exactly what he used to be.

He shrugged. "I guess this ranch is changing me a little."

Her expression shifted from amused to serious as she studied his face. "It looks good on you, Jace."

What would Bonnie do if she knew how close he was to kissing her right now? He could picture her frown and the resolve he knew would replace the relaxed look on her face. She'd probably turn around and walk right to his truck and insist he take her home.

But what if she didn't? What if she wanted to kiss him even a fraction as much as he wanted to kiss her?

"Bonnie...Am I the only one that feels things shifting between us?" When she didn't answer right away, he continued. "I've always admired you. The way you care for Gunner. The way you're not afraid to stand up for something, even if it means arguing with me." That got a little laugh out of her, and she relaxed a bit. "Since we all moved to the ranch, we've had the chance to get to know each other better." He paused, trying to search for the right words. "It's made me wish I hadn't waited this long."

Jace stepped forward and reached out, taking her hand in his. Her soft skin cool to the touch.

Bonnie's gaze went to their hands. He thought she was going to pull hers away, but to his relief, she didn't. "This is a terrible idea."

"Maybe. But what if it's not?" Jace had been questioning things for days now. What if the mistake would be in ignoring how he cared for Bonnie?

"We argue all the time." Bonnie looked up, some of that familiar fire of confrontation flickering in her eyes. "That ought to be a sign."

"I like to think that we challenge each other. Push each other to be better people."

The corners of her mouth pulled up in an amused smile. "I suppose that's one way to look at it." Her smile faltered. "I just don't want to mess anything up here. My job. My friendships with you or Noel. I don't want to lose Gunner."

There was no missing the catch in her voice at the end. Knowing she cared about his son had Jace falling just a little more in love with her still. "You won't lose Gunner. But I do appreciate how much you care about him." He wanted to say how much she cared about all of them but didn't want to push her. They were both tired. Maybe now wasn't the time to bare his heart and ask her to do the same in return. "It's super late. Come on, you need some sleep. I'll drive you back to your place."

He tugged her towards his truck. When she didn't remove her hand from his, he didn't initiate it, either. Instead, he held her hand all the way to the truck and only let go once he'd opened her door and she climbed inside.

The ride back to the house and garage seemed even more quiet with the dark of night surrounding them. Once there, Jace walked her to the door.

She turned to face him. "Thanks for letting me tag along tonight."

"Anytime." He meant that, too. If she could come with him every time he needed to tend to things on the farm, his days would be a whole lot brighter. "Get some rest. You earned it."

She hesitated for a moment before rising onto the toes of her shoes.

To his surprise, she placed a whisper of a kiss on his cheek near the corner of his mouth. The brief touch had his mind spinning as he watched her take a small step back.

Hope flitted across her face quickly followed by doubt. Did she regret the kiss? Because he sure didn't. When her doubt was chased by embarrassment, he realized she took his hesitation for rejection.

She turned away. "Good night, Jace."

She moved to unlock the door, but before she could take the key out of her pocket, Jace reached for her arm.

He gently tugged her toward him again. The moment she lifted her chin, her gaze tangled with his as he leaned in and kissed her.

He'd intended for it to be brief. A peck meant to reassure her that the tiny kiss she'd offered earlier had not only been appreciated but welcome.

When his lips melded with hers, all thoughts of a brief kiss disappeared. All that existed was the way she fit perfectly into his embrace.

Her arm went around his neck. He pulled her closer, deepening their kiss. Everything about it—about her—was like coming home.

Their kiss ended much sooner than he would've liked, and he let his forehead rest against hers. This changed everything, but he didn't come close to regretting it. "Good night, Bonnie."

Bonnie looked like she might say something. Instead, she offered him a shy smile, unlocked the door, and went inside. Just before she closed it again, she lifted a hand in farewell.

Jace waited long enough to hear the lock slide back into place before going into the house. The light was still on in the living room where Noel had crashed on the couch. She sat up quickly and blinked her eyes at him. "Everything go okay? Did the lambs make it?"

"Yep. Both are healthy, and mom is doing great. It's good we were there, though. We had to assist with the first one, but once we did that, the second arrived easily on its own."

"That's a relief. I haven't heard a peep from Gunner since he went to sleep." She stood and stretched her arms over her head. "My bed is calling me." She stopped and squinted at him. A slow smile stole every hint of weariness from her face. "Something else happened tonight, didn't it?"

"Good night, Noel." He tried to hide his grin from her as he moved toward the stairs.

"Good for you," Noel said behind him and then raised her voice. "It's about time!"

Chapter Sixteen

Bonnie had no idea what to expect when she showed up at the main house for work the next day. But the knowing look from Noel told her that the woman had at least guessed about the kiss between Bonnie and Jace, or Jace had told her. Either way, heat infused Bonnie's cheeks as she tried to act normal.

"Jace is already out working with Cabe," Noel said as she gathered her things. "Gunner was hungry early, so I fed him some breakfast. He is super energetic today." She grabbed her bag and slung it over her shoulder. "I guess Jace talked to Cabe first thing this morning. The mama and two babies are doing well."

That brought a smile to Bonnie's face. "That's great to hear." She wondered if it'd be okay to go to the barn in the next day or two and see the lambs. "My parents were against pets. I never experienced something like that before. It was amazing."

"My brother feels the same way, though I'm sure it isn't just the lambing." Noel smiled at Bonnie with a mischievous glint in her eye. "I'm happy for you guys. You know, in case my opinion matters." She winked. "I'll see you this evening. Have a great day, Bonnie."

"Yeah, you too."

The front door closed, and it was several moments before Bonnie moved to slide the deadbolt into place. Gunner pushed his toy car into the room, complete with all kinds of motor sounds and spit to accompany them.

She greeted the boy, but her mind was centered on the man who was somewhere else on the property. Just thinking about him had her lips tingling at the memory of their kisses.

She worried all morning about what it would be like to talk to him this morning. Did the kisses mean as much to him as they did to her? Would things be weird between them? Would he act as though nothing had changed? Is that how she was supposed to act?

Now she simply wished he'd been at the house when she arrived. Then she'd have some answers to all of her neurotic questions.

Well, she had a job to do and a little boy to spend time with. There was no sense in acting like a twitterpated schoolgirl.

The decision made, she checked on Gunner and then tackled the kitchen.

She'd only been working twenty minutes when her phone pinged. Jace's name brought a smile to her lips.

"Sorry I missed you this morning. I'll try to stop by at lunch. Have a good morning."

It was a simple text, but knowing she was on his mind made Bonnie's day. "I'll look forward to it. Don't work too hard today."

All she got in response was a smiley face, but it was enough to keep her cheerful for most of the morning.

She'd been afraid the time would drag, but between her extensive to-do list plus Gunner, it went by pretty quickly.

The moment she heard Jace's boots on the front porch, Bonnie smoothed her hair and took in a deep breath.

"Just act like a normal person, Bonnie."

She knew when he entered the living room because Gunner ran by yelling out, "Daddy!"

Jace scooped his son into his arms and hugged him close. His gaze sought out Bonnie's and rested on her face.

She raised a hand in greeting. "Hey. Did your morning go okay?"

"Yep. It's been super busy. The new lambs are doing well, though." He set his son down and put a stack of envelopes on a nearby table. "I'm glad you insisted on helping me with them last night." He took a step closer and reached for her hand.

Bonnie's breath caught. "I am, too."

"Maybe I could take you out this weekend. We could go into Clearwater, get some dinner. You know, without a certain little boy or newborn lambs to act as distractions." Jace chuckled.

Her smile widened. "Are you asking me out on a date, cowboy?"

"Yes, ma'am, I am." He traced an invisible pattern on the back of her hand with his thumb.

"I'd like that." Warmth spread through her at the thought of going out on a date with Jace.

Her gaze wandered to the stack of envelopes he had set down. Her heart stalled as she recognized the handwriting on the top envelope. "Oh no."

Jace looked confused. "What's wrong?"

She lifted the envelope with her free hand. "This is from my parents." Why would they be contacting Jace? The handwriting wasn't her mom's—Bonnie wasn't sure if Mom had ever addressed an envelope herself. But there was no missing the swooping letters of their housekeeper because Nell had been handling Mom's mail for years.

Jace glanced at her, curiosity filling his expression. He let go of her hand and broke the fancy seal on the back. As he slid an invitation out, Bonnie's stomach fell to her feet.

"It's a birthday party invitation. For your birthday party." A smile tugged at the corners of his mouth until he must have realized just how unhappy she was about it.

What made them think they could just invite anyone they wanted to the party? It was supposed to be her party—not that she wanted one. This gathering, like everything else, was all about her mom having the chance to show off her status in the town of Clearwater.

Bonnie snatched the invitation from his hand. "Yeah, trust me, you don't want to go to that."

Jace withdrew another envelope. "Looks like Noel got one, too."

Bonnie groaned.

Jace's brows drew together. "I take it this party isn't your idea."

"Nope. It never is. In fact, every year I ask that we *not* have a party. You can see how well that request goes over."

"I'm sorry. Well, you met my mother. Trust me, I get it." His gaze roamed over the wording on the invitation. "It's this Friday evening. You have to go, right?"

Bonnie nodded, slightly amused by the phrasing of his question. "Yes, unfortunately."

"So if I happen to show up, you'll have one more person in your corner. Surely that can't be all bad. I can even give you a ride."

She wanted to tell him no, but he looked at her with a soft expression that nearly melted away her resolve.

It would be good to have someone besides Wyatt and Chrissy there who would have her back. If he went, though, he'd be playing right into the game her mother had set up.

"It's a test, Jace." When he looked confused, she elaborated. "If you were simply my employer, there's no way you'd come to my birthday party. Think about it. Did you ever get an invitation from her before? I've had two other birthdays since I started working for you. If you do go with me—or even show up separately—my mom is going to infer that it means I'm more than just your employee."

An intense need to protect Jace—and Gunner—from her parents' criticism hit her like a blow.

She hadn't realized how transparent her thoughts were until Jace touched her chin with one finger and lifted it until she was looking into his eyes.

"You are more than just my employee." The smile he offered her was so sweet that it made her heart ache. "Besides, I can take care of myself." He softened his words with a wink. "Unless you genuinely don't want me to go, I'd like to celebrate your birthday with you."

Bonnie focused on the warmth of his finger and the way his other hand went around her waist to rest against her back.

There were a lot of reasons why she should tell him not to go. Except she couldn't imagine anyone else she'd rather spend a horribly awkward evening with.

"Just don't say I didn't warn you."

"I wouldn't dare."

With that, he pulled her close and kissed her until the doubts that remained were easily ignored.

ANY CONFIDENCE BONNIE POSSESSED DISAPPEARED THE moment they drove through the ranch's gate Friday evening. She didn't realize how tense she was until Jace placed a hand over hers—a hand that clutched the edge of her seat as though clinging for her life.

He cradled her hand in his. "Relax. What's the worst that could happen tonight?"

She shot him a severe look. "Let's not even play that game." With a great deal of effort, she released the air she'd been holding and made herself relax against the back of her seat.

There were many ways the evening could go badly. She tried to center her attention on how warm the skin of his hand felt against her own. How the simple action was like a calming balm that slowly spread through her nervous system until she could almost imagine them going on a picnic or somewhere peaceful. Almost.

He must have sensed her need to focus on something because he changed the topic to Joyful Hope Stables. A topic Bonnie was always happy to talk about.

"I still can't believe that, by building the stables, your brother was cut off from your family's money." Jace shook his head.

"Oh, you can believe it." She cast him a sideways glance. "But the whole topic is taboo, just so you know. I figured I'd give you a heads up since you're determined to torture yourself by coming with me to this shindig."

"Don't talk about the family money. Got it. Any other topics I should steer clear of?" He glanced at her, humor dancing in his eyes.

"Politics. Other people's money. I'd like to say you shouldn't bring me up in conversation, but given it's my birthday party, I'm not sure there's a lot of choice there." She released a deep sigh. "Let's just say I half hoped I'd wake up with a cold or the flu or something. I might have done a back-flip because I'd legitimately have a reason to bail if that tells you anything."

To his credit, he didn't try to convince her the party wouldn't be as bad as she thought it would.

"Well, I'm glad you didn't wake up sick this morning. Maybe I'm being selfish, but I would've missed getting to spend the day with you. Even if it is in combination with the rest of your family." He kissed her hand before releasing it. "Wyatt is clearly happy with his decision to walk away from your family's money. But what about you? Do you ever regret it?"

She thought about his question a moment. "Truthfully? No. I don't. But it frustrates me because my parents continue to build this huge stockpile of money they like to flaunt. If I had it, or if Wyatt had it, there's so much good we could do. Wyatt, especially, with the stables. There are many people that could benefit by what he does here." She shrugged. "It's a shame, you know?"

"Yeah, I know what you mean." Jace remained silent for several heartbeats.

He came from a wealthy family and had a great deal of money himself, from what Bonnie knew. Did he think she was criticizing his use of it? She sure hoped not. "What you are doing with the ranch is admirable, Jace. You're giving Gunner something he can learn from and hold on to. That's priceless." It was time to change the subject. "It was kind of Noel to stay with Gunner."

Jace nodded. "Although she's super curious about your family." He gave her an amused smile. "I'm pretty sure she's going to demand a full report from me when I get home again."

Bonnie had no doubt about that. "I'm sorry she wasn't able to come. I would've liked that, but I didn't want Gunner to be uncomfortable."

"There won't be any other kids at the party?" His eyebrows rose.

"There will be, but they are expected to be seen and not heard. My mom will have a room all set up for them to stay. They'll watch a movie and eat their own food until it's time for cake. Once I've blown out the candles as expected, they'll be escorted back again." Bonnie remembered being a kid during these celebrations. At the time, she didn't care because it was a chance to play with cousins and eat sweets. But looking back, it was clearly just another example of how she and her siblings were considered an inconvenience.

"That's sad." He paused. "Gunner will be happier at home. Besides, I can focus on spending time with you and acting as your human shield."

That coaxed a laugh from Bonnie. "You only think you're joking…"

"We've got this. Together."

The gentle way in which he said that last word had Bonnie's heart stuttering. She glanced at him to find Jace smiling at her. He took her hand again and squeezed it gently.

Together. She liked the sound of that.

It didn't take nearly long enough to drive to her parents' home in Clearwater. When Jace followed the line of cars to the front of the house, they were met by a valet who offered to take the keys.

Jace handed them over. Moments later, he and Bonnie stood in front of the house. "So this is it?"

"Uh-huh. If we start running now, we could probably make it home again before breakfast."

He laughed loudly at that and placed a hand against her back. "Come on, birthday girl." In his other hand, he produced a brightly wrapped box. When she gave him a surprised look, he chuckled again. "You didn't think I'd come to a birthday party unprepared, did you?"

Bonnie didn't have long to wonder at his thoughtfulness because the moment they arrived at the door, Bonnie was swept into the middle of the crowd. Out of nowhere, Mom was there whispering fiercely into Bonnie's ear. "You're late."

"I'm not late. You said the party was at three. I'm ten minutes early."

Mom squeezed Bonnie's upper arm harder than necessary. "You know I like the guest of honor to be here at least a half hour before the event begins. It's polite for you to greet the guests as they arrive." The last two words were cut short as she smiled and immediately started to whisk Bonnie around the room as though she were showing off her most recent art procurement.

Bonnie glanced behind her to catch a glimpse of Jace. He gave her a sympathetic look as Wyatt walked up to greet him.

At least she didn't have to worry as much about Jace since he had an ally in his corner now.

Bonnie quickly lost count of how many people she'd hugged, greeted, and smiled at. Truth be told, she only recognized half of them. It wasn't until Gran linked arms with her that Bonnie was no longer dragged around the room.

"I want to visit with my granddaughter. Come sit down with me, Bonnie."

Bonnie was more than happy to oblige. She sank into the sofa next to Gran. "Thanks." She lowered her voice. "I owe you one."

"I have no idea what you're talking about." Gran patted her on the knee with a sparkle in her eye. "By the way, I have every intention of taking you out for a birthday dinner during your next available evening."

Bonnie grinned at her. "I'd like that."

"Good." Gran gave a single nod indicating that the matter was settled. "Now where is that handsome young man of yours? It's so nice of him to escort you to the party." She craned her neck until she spotted Jace and Wyatt across the room. "He's one of the good ones. I can tell, you know."

"Yeah, I know." Bonnie smiled and then had to cover a cringe when Mom walked between them and Jace. Bonnie truly doubted Mom would agree with them, though. Then again, he was rich. That was probably the biggest thing on Mom's list of what it took to be worthy of her daughter.

Bonnie was able to visit with Gran and a couple other family members for several minutes before Mom took control of the party and ushered everyone into the large, fancy dining room that was only used for entertaining guests.

To her relief, Jace appeared to her left and Wyatt to her right followed by Chrissy. They sat down together before Mom could direct their seating arrangements. The men were almost like guards on either side, and Bonnie was grateful for it.

Once everyone had been seated, Bonnie's parents stood at the head of the table. Dad cleared his throat. "Thank you all for coming to help us celebrate Bonnie's birthday today."

Mom nodded, a wide smile on her face that Bonnie had long ago dubbed Mom's public smile. "We hope you enjoy lunch today. We have a variety of sushi available in Bonnie's honor. For those of you who require dietary alternatives, please speak with one of the servers who will be happy to help you with that."

Bonnie resisted the urge to roll her eyes. In her honor? Right. Mom knew she hated sushi. Bonnie would love to speak with one of the servers about an alternative, but that wouldn't go over well at all. See, this is when they needed a family dog—preferably one that liked to eat sushi that just happened to disappear under the dinner table...

Jace's arm rested against the back of her chair and his hand on her shoulder. He leaned in close and whispered,

"We'll swing by and grab a burger on the way back to the ranch."

Bonnie hid her smile behind her hand and gave what she hoped was a discreet nod. "Bless you."

She managed to choke down some sushi thanks to two glasses of water and a great deal of hope that there would be some form of chocolate for dessert.

The actual food aside, Bonnie enjoyed visiting with Jace, Wyatt, Chrissy, and some of the other people around her. When everyone had finished eating, they were all escorted back to the sitting room where gifts were waiting on a nearby table.

Bonnie swallowed hard. She always hated that everyone attending felt obligated to bring a gift. Especially when most of them didn't even know her. But took a seat on the sofa and began to open them, being sure to thank each individual for their gift.

The wrapped box from Wyatt and Chrissy contained a purple blouse Bonnie had admired the last time she and Chrissy went shopping. She ran a hand over the soft fabric. "It's beautiful. Thank you both."

She recognized the next gift brought to her and gave Jace a shy smile. She carefully opened the square box and then gasped in surprise when she withdrew a bracelet complete with two charms: a guinea pig and a lamb.

"This is perfect. Thank you." She held her out her arm so that he could put the bracelet on her wrist. Remembering the guinea pig was thoughtful. And the lamb? It reminded her of helping Jace in the barn, and that brought to mind their first kiss. It was the perfect gift. Her gaze met his and she gave him a smile she hoped relayed how much she liked it.

When all of the other gifts had been opened, her parents came forward with a small, red envelope. Dad handed it to her. "Happy birthday, sweetheart."

Bonnie smiled as she took it. She slid a finger underneath the flap and pulled two pieces of paper out. The first was a gift certificate to the salon and spa at the country club her family owned. The other was a check for way more money than anyone should give someone else for their birthday. She forced what she hoped looked like a genuine smile. "Thank you both so much." She stood and gave them a hug.

Because Mom couldn't stand others not knowing about her "generosity," she announced, "A spa day and mad money —what more could a girl want?"

There were a lot of chuckles around the room along with a number of women who nodded enthusiastically.

Bonnie wasn't the spa type. Instead of voicing her thoughts, she slid the papers back into the envelope and carefully placed it in another box at her feet. "You are way too kind. Thank you."

Before she'd had a chance to do anything, her mom waved a hand and someone cleared the gifts, moving them to another room where they would be boxed up and placed in the car for her to take home. Thankfully, someone had also written everything down and who it was from like you would at a baby shower so that she could send out thank you notes. Something Bonnie would normally do anyway.

Dad stood again. "Why don't we head out to the back patio. We have drinks and dessert waiting."

Everyone headed that way, but Bonnie hung back until Jace paused next to her. "You really like the bracelet?"

"Yeah, I do. It's beautiful." She looked into his face and wished she could kiss him right then. "Thank you again."

"You're welcome." He smiled at her. "You ready for dessert?"

Bonnie's stomach rumbled a response. "Oh, yeah."

He offered her an arm and she'd just slipped her hand into the crook of his elbow when Mom came up behind them.

"Bonnie, dear, you should get outside and mingle with the guests. They are here for you."

"Jace is a guest, too." The words were out before she could stop them. She placed a smile on her face that would hopefully soften them. "I just wanted to thank him for the thoughtful birthday gift. We were on our way out."

Mom gave Jace a long look, and it was one that Bonnie couldn't quite decipher. "I'm glad you came today, Jace. I appreciate your willingness to escort my daughter."

Bonnie bit back a response. That Mom insinuated Bonnie needed an escort–and only saw Jace as that–annoyed her to no end.

Bonnie snagged Jace's arm and gently pulled him in the direction of the patio outside. When they were out of earshot, she leaned closer and whispered fiercely, "She drives me insane."

"I have to admit that today hasn't been as bad as I thought it could be after everything you've said." When he spoke, he leaned in close enough that his breath brushed against her ear. She suppressed a shiver.

"Oh, the day isn't over with. My parents are all smiles when guests are here. They'll expect us to stay until everyone has left, and then it's a whole different game."

"So what you're saying is we should sneak out the back door before the rest of the guests leave…"

The mischievous look on his face had her giggling. "We will definitely keep that plan in mind."

She was glad Jace had come with her. She'd had her doubts when he'd insisted on attending her birthday party, and her parents' behavior was on the top of that list. But standing here with him, joking about the day…it was almost scary, but she could easily get used to this.

Chapter Seventeen

Birthday dessert on the patio went well. At least Mom had arranged for chocolate cake along with several other choices. Bonnie wandered through the guests and spoke to most of them. And when it was time for everyone to leave, she made sure to stand by the front door and thank each of them for coming.

Bonnie wished Wyatt and Chrissy would stay longer, but Dad rushed them out the door shortly after Bonnie hugged them both goodbye. That left her and Jace with her parents. A situation she hadn't been looking forward to.

Mom reached out and smoothed some of Bonnie's hair back into place. "Come with me, Bonnie. We need to sort through your gifts and get them in the car for you."

Bonnie looked back at Jace, hoping he would join them. The last thing she wanted to do was leave him here with Dad alone.

As though Mom knew what was on Bonnie's mind, she said, "We'll let the guys talk. We won't be long."

What were the odds they could box up the gifts in comfortable silence?

The moment they entered the sitting room where the gifts

had been taken, Bonnie noted that they were already packed neatly in boxes and ready to go.

Mom turned and fixed Bonnie with one of her serious looks. The kind that meant she intended Bonnie to listen and pay attention.

"You're thirty-two now, Bonnie. It's time to grow up."

Mom's tactless comment had Bonnie speechless. "Excuse me?"

"You've been playing nanny in the Echolls household for over two years. Do you have any idea how that looks? Jace Echolls is one of the richest men in town, after your father of course, and no eligible man is going to offer you his hand in marriage while you're still connected to the Echolls family." Mom folded her hands in front of her as though she were reciting some kind of poetry instead of making Bonnie feel as though she'd just turned a hundred years old or something.

"What would you have me do? Quit my job and sign up for the first online dating site I run into? Stand on the street corner with a sign announcing that I'm in the market for a husband? What makes you think I want to get married in the first place?"

Mom looked at Bonnie as though she'd grown a third eye right in the middle of her forehead. "Don't be ridiculous, Bonnie. Really." She released a heavy sigh as though she'd been forced to carry a burden for far too long. "You need to quit playing around and marry Jace Echolls."

"Excuse me?" Bonnie's voice has risen an octave even to her own ears. Her mom had overstepped bounds before. Many times. But this? This was way too much. Anger that she'd often experienced with regards to her parents boiled up. Her chest ached. How many times had she been criticized and told she was living her life wrong? How many times had she ignored her parents' words in order to keep the peace?

This conversation needed to end before she said something she might regret later.

"Look, I should go and let you and Dad have some time to relax after the party. Thank you again for all the effort you put into it."

She moved to pick up a box of gifts, but Mom shifted to stand between Bonnie and the table. "You're hiding out at that ranch like some mistress who is ashamed of who she is. Marry Jace Echolls. You'll finally have access to the money you deserve, Bonnie. The money you should've had by now if you weren't so blasted stubborn."

Bonnie's hands clenched and she straightened her spine. "I'm all grown up now, Mom. I don't need your money." She lifted her chin as her body tensed. "You married Dad for money. It's worked out for you guys, and I'm glad you're happy together. But I'll never marry money. Stop trying to push Jace at me, Mom. I'm not going to marry some rich man just to help you align yourself with one of the richest families in Clearwater. I wish you could see I'm doing fine on my own." With that, Bonnie whirled to walk out of the room.

She stopped short, her heart jumping into her throat when she saw Dad and Jace standing in the doorway.

Dad's face was as red as a tomato. But Jace? His eyes were void of emotion and his lips pressed together as he watched her.

How much had he heard?

After Bonnie and her mother left, Jace had tried to ignore every one of his instincts that screamed at him to go with them. Instead, he turned to Mr. Tabor in an attempt to be polite. If Jace's hopes for the future came about, he'd have to learn how to get along with the man one way or another. "It was a great party, sir. Thank you again for inviting me to join in the celebration." He held a hand out.

Mr. Tabor shook it, but then didn't let go immediately. Instead, he glanced in the direction the women had gone and lowered his voice. "You seem like a bright young man. Surely, now that you've seen where Bonnie comes from, you can understand why she deserves more than to simply work and care for your son."

"I assure you, sir, that I both pay and treat her well. She isn't just an employee. We are a team, and we make a good one." Jace paused as he tried to choose his words carefully. "Bonnie is an amazing woman with a strong personality. We both know that, if she didn't want to work as my son's nanny, no one would be able to stop her from quitting."

"The fact that she's working a menial job at all shows her judgment could be better." Mr. Tabor pinned Jace with a look full of accusation. "Marry my daughter, Mr. Echolls, or cut her free. But do not enable what has amounted to a lifetime of bad choices on her behalf."

Mr. Tabor wanted Jace to marry Bonnie? That was the last thing he'd expected to hear when he came to the party tonight. But to say that hiring Bonnie as his nanny was enabling her bad choices? It took several moments for Jace to digest that a father could speak so poorly of his own daughter. He couldn't fathom speaking about Gunner in such a way.

He'd been on the receiving end of criticism and disappointment. Bonnie didn't deserve to be treated like this.

Jace clenched his jaw to keep from saying what he really wanted to voice and took a moment to contain his anger. When he did speak, he was careful to keep his tone even. "I believe it's time for Bonnie and me to go." Without waiting for permission, he headed in the direction Bonnie went a few minutes earlier.

He heard the women's raised voices before he saw them.

So Mrs. Tabor had been pushing her daughter as well. Anger burned. Bonnie's voice rose more, and he wanted to cheer her on for sticking up for herself. Until he was close enough to hear the conversation.

"But I'll never marry money. Stop trying to push Jace at me, Mom. I'm not going to marry some rich man just to help you align yourself with one of the richest families in Clearwater. I wish you could see I'm doing fine on my own."

Bonnie's words slammed into him as a knot formed in his stomach. He tried to swallow, but his parched throat wouldn't cooperate.

After what Mr. Tabor had said, Jace could only imagine the unkind words Mrs. Tabor might've had for Bonnie. He wanted to believe that Bonnie hadn't meant what she just said, or that he'd somehow heard it all out of context.

He had no doubt she loved Gunner. He'd never gotten the impression she didn't want to work for him, even when they butted heads.

But what if Bonnie had just spoken from the heart? What if she was too stubborn to accept someone that her parents wanted her to marry? If her parents didn't want her to be a nanny in the first place, was Bonnie really staying with him and Gunner because it's what she genuinely wanted? Or was she doing it because she was rebelling against what her parents wanted for her?

If that's how Bonnie felt, then what was he doing? Was Bonnie capable of a relationship that her parents might actually approve of?

Bonnie turned and saw him, as well as her father, standing in the doorway. Immediately, her eyes widened, and a combination of determination and remorse crossed her features. She bit her bottom lip.

They needed to talk, but not here. Right now, he needed to get Bonnie out of her parents' house. He strode forward, put a protective arm around her shoulders, and said, "It's time we got back to the ranch."

She nodded silently. Not a single word was spoken in the room as they left, closing the front door behind them. The man outside scrambled to get Jace's truck and bring it around to the front.

Once he and Bonnie were inside and he'd pulled away from the house, everything started to sink in. He glanced at Bonnie and noted a drop of blood on her lip where she'd bitten it before.

He withdrew a handkerchief and handed it to her. "For your lip."

She took it and dabbed at the small cut. "Thanks."

They drove in silence until they reached the Clearwater city limits.

When Bonnie spoke again, her voice soft making it difficult to hear her words over the sound of the engine. "I'm sorry you went through that, Jace. I should've insisted you not go to the party. I should've refused to go myself. I knew better."

That's the part she was sorry for? He swallowed hard. "They never should've spoken to you like they did." He paused. "But did you mean what you said back there? About not wanting to marry someone rich?" Not wanting to marry him? The fact that she didn't respond immediately only confirmed his fear. "I'd like to hope I've proven I'm nothing like your parents. Mine, either."

"Of course you're nothing like either of them. It isn't about you, it's all about me. My parents are wrong about a lot of things. But maybe Mom has been right when she's insisted that I only went from relying on them to relying on you. If we... I'd just be trading one fortune for another, Jace. That isn't fair to you."

He couldn't have this conversation while driving. He

pulled onto a wide shoulder and turned to look at her. "You aren't giving yourself enough credit, Bonnie. You've worked hard for what you make watching Gunner. That's all on you, that isn't because of anything your parents are doing, or anything I've done." He ran his fingers through his hair and pulled a little on the ends. "I have a lot of money, but I'm not going to apologize for that. I've worked hard for it. If you have an issue with that…"

Bonnie only shook her head and pressed a hand against her forehead.

"Talk to me, Bonnie."

"Things are way too complicated, Jace." Something about the way the light in her eyes changed had Jace's heart clenching in pain. "I need some time to figure things out."

"You need to figure things out about your job? Or us?" He braced himself, unsure he even wanted to know the answer.

"Maybe both." She was looking down at her hands. Slowly, her long lashes lifted revealing eyes full of unshed tears.

Confusion mixed with anger. "I can't go back to being just friends." He wanted to tell her he loved her but couldn't quite get the words out.

"Meaning what, Jace?" A single tear escaped, effectively breaking his heart.

"Meaning maybe we both need to figure things out."

Her jaws clenched and the sadness in her eyes was quickly replaced with anger. "Can we just go home please?"

"Yep." He put the truck in drive and got back up on the highway. The rest of the way to the ranch was silent. Jace clenched the steering wheel until his hand ached and his knuckles turned white.

When they reached the driveway in front of the house,

Jace parked, prepared to walk her the rest of the way to her apartment.

She wasted no time in releasing her seatbelt and getting out of the truck. She was halfway to the walkway by the time he got out as well.

"Bonnie!"

"You're not going to have to worry about being friends, Jace. You can expect my two-week notice on your desk Monday morning."

With that, she disappeared from sight, leaving Jace standing in the driveway staring after her.

His head pounded, and he didn't know whether he wanted to run after her and yell some sense into her more or kiss her until she finally admitted that they belonged together.

Instead, he ascended the steps to the front door where he met Noel as she opened it.

"What on earth is going on out here? I heard the two of you yelling at each other all the way from the kitchen." Noel's eyes searched his face. "Are you okay?"

"Nope."

She frowned. "I take it that it wasn't just the party."

"Nope." He wasn't in the mood to talk and tried to push past his sister anyway.

But Noel grabbed his arm on the way past. "What happened, Jace?"

His shoulders dropped as the weight of what that meant hit him squarely in the chest. "I think I'm losing her."

Chapter Eighteen

"You're losing her? Like she's quitting so you can be together without complications? Or like she's moving to England because she hates your guts?" Noel stared at Jace, clearly confused.

"Something in between." He sighed. "She said she's going to give her two-week notice on Monday." He wasn't in the mood to talk about this right now. "How did Gunner do? Is he asleep?"

Noel's eyes widened as though she couldn't believe her ears. "Gunner? Yeah, he did fine. He's fast asleep." She shook her head. "I knew I should've gone to the party, too," she muttered. "What do you mean? She's quitting? What are you doing standing here?" Noel motioned to the front door. "Go talk to her. Tell her you love her. Convince her to stay."

"She doesn't want me." The words stung, and the weight of what they meant sat on his chest like a boulder.

"Okay, you have got to tell me what happened." Noel grabbed his arm and steered him to the couch. She waited for him to sit before joining him. "I've seen the way Bonnie looks at you. I'm about as sure she's in love with you as you are with her. One stressful afternoon doesn't erase that or the last two years you've spent getting to know each other."

Jace replayed the conversation he'd overheard in his mind. He wanted to find another way to interpret it, but he couldn't. He took a deep breath, let it out slowly, and then told his sister everything about the birthday party.

She remained silent, but the reactions on her face spoke of her shock at how rude Bonnie's parents had been, her happiness at the way Bonnie reacted to the bracelet, and then her confusion and hurt over what he heard Bonnie say to her mother.

"I can't believe she'd say something like that. Maybe you misheard or misunderstood her?"

Jace shook his head. "I don't think so. In the truck, she told me that she'd only be trading her family's money for mine. And that she needed time to figure things out." He went over what he'd said and frowned. "I might have told her I couldn't go back to being just friends." It'd be incredibly difficult to set aside his feelings for her and return to friend status after getting a taste of what a relationship with her would be like.

He groaned, and Noel kicked him in the shin. "Well, that was a stupid thing to say. Or at the very least, one of the worst times to say it."

He rubbed his shin. "You're not wrong. But I can't unsay it, either."

Noel crossed her arms in front of her. "I still think you should go over and talk to her."

"She said she needed time. I'm going to give it to her. And maybe she's not the only one." He let his hands hit his knees and then stood. "Bonnie's stubborn. No one can tell her what to do. She'll have to make up her own mind." He headed toward the staircase.

"She's not the only one who's stubborn," Noel muttered as she got to her feet and followed him. "Did you hear me?"

"Yep." He was tired of talking. "Look, I'm going to check on Gunner and then work in the office for a while." He engulfed his sister in a hug. "Thanks for watching Gunner for me this evening. I appreciate you."

"You're welcome." Her voice was muffled against his shirt. "I'm sorry today wasn't better."

He gave her a smile that he hoped reassured her at least somewhat. After he peeked in on Gunner and pressed a kiss to his son's cheek, he grabbed the baby monitor and headed back downstairs. He'd just entered the living room again when headlights caught his attention. He pulled back the curtains to see Bonnie's car driving away from the house.

It was nearly nine o'clock. He sure wished he knew whether she was going into town for something or staying somewhere else for the night.

What he needed was a distraction and going over the financial books for the ranch was a good one. Besides, he was already in a foul mood. Seeing how much they'd lost with the stolen sheep wasn't going to make it much worse. Jace sank into his office chair and leaned back to stare at the ceiling. All thoughts of going over finances fled his mind as his thought kept churning through everything that had happened. How could he go from being blissful and positive about his future to losing the woman he loved in the span of a day?

He rested his elbows on the desk and his forehead in his hands. "What am I supposed to do now?" he prayed.

§

IT WAS SATURDAY MORNING, AND BONNIE WAS SICK OF crying. Her eyes ached, and her nose was in a state of permanent stuffiness. She stretched her arms above her head and hit the arm of the futon she'd slept on last night.

Wyatt and Chrissy were so sweet. Not only did they let her stay with them for the weekend, but she'd been so exhausted when she arrived last night that they hadn't pressed her for information. Instead, they'd made sure she had everything she needed, wished her goodnight, and then gave her space.

Space to cry. Space to feel rotten and wonder why everything happened the way it did. And then space to pray. She hadn't received any perfect answer about what to do, but she had received some peace and sleep, both of which she'd desperately needed.

Bonnie looked around the spare bedroom. Wyatt and Chrissy had been using it as a combination study and storage room, although she knew they were eventually going to clean it out and use it as a nursery. That thought brought another round of pain as she thought about their loss.

Sounds coming from the kitchen told her at least one of them was already awake. She got up, grabbed some clothes from the small bag she'd packed, and went to the bathroom to change and clean up.

A few minutes later, she entered the kitchen, the linoleum cool to her bare feet. Wyatt sat at the table with a cup of coffee while Chrissy stirred eggs in a frying pan.

"Good morning," Wyatt greeted. "Did you sleep okay? I know the futon isn't the most comfortable bed around."

Bonnie gave him a reassuring smile. "As soon as my head hit the pillow, I was out. Thank you both for letting me stay here for the weekend."

"You know you're welcome anytime." Wyatt stood and pulled her into a hug. He pointed to Oreo whose cage was resting on the bar connecting the living room with the kitchen. "Although she should consider herself privileged."

Bonnie chuckled. Yeah, she'd looked pretty ridiculous trying to load the large cage into her car. But she couldn't just leave the poor guinea pig at the apartment for two days without veggies. Oreo was snoozing in her house, one eye half open. "Don't worry, we'll be out of your hair Sunday evening."

In the case that Jace accepted her two-week notice without firing her on the spot, Bonnie had considered staying elsewhere and driving to work every morning. Except it wasn't practical, especially since all of her things were on the ranch.

She needed to deal with whatever the next two weeks brought, knowing that it would all be over soon.

Her thoughts shifted to Jace. There was a big part of her that'd hoped he would follow her to the apartment.

If he'd wanted her to stay, he would've tried to convince her. Even if it meant continuing their argument. Instead, he'd just let her go.

The thought of quitting her job, leaving the ranch, and not seeing him or Gunner, hurt more than she wanted to admit. Would he hire another nanny and expect Bonnie to do some of the training? Let her stay on for those two weeks? Or when she handed in her notice, would he dismiss her right then?

Ugh, and finding a place to live. That was going to be fun. Not.

"Bonnie?"

The sound of Chrissy's voice snagged Bonnie's attention, and from the look on her and Wyatt's faces, she gathered she must have missed something. "I'm sorry. Did you say something?"

Chrissy flashed her a sympathetic look. "Would you like some eggs and orange juice?"

Bonnie's stomach growled in response. "I'd love some,

thank you." She took a seat at the table. She and Jace never did get those burgers they'd planned on after the party.

A fresh wave of sorrow hit her, and she willed the building tears away.

Maybe she was thinking about all of this the wrong way, and she should be relieved this happened sooner rather than later. Because as much as she wanted everything to work out between her and Jace, there was that underlying fear that they'd end up like her parents. Or even his. As far as Bonnie was concerned, money caused way more problems than it fixed.

Chrissy set a plate in front of her along with a glass of orange juice.

"Thank you." She waited until they were seated with their food before she took the first bite. The moment she swallowed it, she nodded appreciatively. "This tastes amazing. I haven't had anything since the party." She made a face. "Can you believe they served sushi?"

Wyatt laughed then. "You've hated sushi since the first time you had it."

"I know!" Bonnie shook her head in wonder. "Next year, I'm going to put together my own birthday party and then invite *them*. That way we can have something normal like burgers or pizza." She paused. "Either that or just be out of town. That sounds even better." What had her parents done with her gifts she'd left behind? The only gift she'd been able to take with her was the bracelet Jace gave her. She'd agonized over whether to wear it again this morning or not. She looked down at the charms dangling from her wrist which only brought another wave of emotion.

"What happened, Bonnie?"

The question came from Wyatt. All she'd told them was that she and Jace had a big argument and she needed a place to crash for the weekend. But they deserved to know more.

With her resolve not to cry firmly in place, she related the events at their parents' house after Wyatt and Chrissy left and then the argument in the truck, ending with her telling Jace she'd be turning in her two-week notice on Monday.

Throughout, Wyatt kept shaking his head, his expression more and more annoyed. "Mom is a real piece of work. It was your birthday. The least she could've done was keep it civil and held her tongue for one day."

Chrissy agreed. "As for you and Jace, everyone argues. Trust me." She reached for Wyatt's hand and gave him a private and knowing smile. She turned her attention back to Bonnie. "But it doesn't mean the two of you can't work things out."

In theory.

Bonnie shrugged. "Or maybe I've read way too much into what's happened over the last couple of weeks. Maybe this is a sign that I'm supposed to pick myself up, move on, and find something else to do with my life." Grief crashed into her, causing a fresh wave of tears she fought to contain.

Wyatt handed her a tissue. "Do you honestly believe that?"

Bonnie shrugged and blew her nose.

What if Jace, Gunner, and even the ranch were exactly what she needed and wanted? What if the feeling wasn't mutual?

Wyatt practically inhaled his breakfast. He rested the fork on his plate. "You and Jace both have a lot of history behind you. He's dealing with his own stuff, just like you are. You can't control that. But what you can do is clean out your own proverbial closet. Sweep away the things that are holding you back. Then at least you can honestly say you've done everything you could."

Bonnie stared at him in amazement before looking at Chrissy. "He's way too smart for his own good sometimes."

"Oh, I know." Chrissy playfully slapped his shoulder. "He's also right more often than I'd like to admit, too."

Wyatt pulled her down to sit on his lap and gave her a kiss.

Bonnie watched them, a smile on her face. "I want this with someone. You know? Someone I can laugh with and be myself. Someone who gets me." She saw Jace clearly in her mind and could easily picture the two of them being there for each other in the good and the bad. "I want this with Jace, you guys."

Neither of them looked surprised, but they both seemed relieved that she'd come to that conclusion.

Chrissy pressed a kiss to her husband's chin before standing up and addressing Bonnie. "So what are you going to do?"

Wyatt was right: Some spring cleaning was in order. Her breakfast forgotten, Bonnie got to her feet. "I'm going to go talk to Mom and Dad. There are a few things that need to be said, plus some captive birthday gifts I need to rescue."

Her mind spun with what she wanted to tell them until she looked down and took in her appearance. She wrinkled her nose. "Okay, maybe I'll shower first." She turned to leave the kitchen when her phone pinged, sending her heart rate through the roof.

She glanced at the screen and disappointment hit when she saw Noel's name instead of Jace's. She told Wyatt and Chrissy who it was from before reading the message.

"Hey, Bonnie. I'm worried about you. Are you okay?"

Even though she'd hoped it was Jace, Noel's kindness made Bonnie feel a little better. "I'm staying with my brother, but I'll be back Sunday night."

"I'm glad you'll be back. I'm praying for you and Jace."

Bonnie smiled a little. "I appreciate it." She added a heart emoji and then slid the phone into her pocket. She wanted to ask how Jace was doing but didn't want to put Noel in the middle of everything. Besides, she'd told Jace she needed space and that was exactly what he was giving her. She couldn't fault him for that, even if she wished he'd reach out.

Chapter Nineteen

❦

Jace woke up Sunday morning. One of the first things he did was look out the alcove window. When the driveway sat empty, disappointment settled in his chest like a stone. She must have stayed at her brother's house, at least that's what he was hoping for. He resisted the temptation to call her and make sure she was okay.

He yawned and stretched with a groan. For the amount of time he'd sat awake in his office, he'd gotten little done. He couldn't take his mind off Bonnie or their last conversation. Even when he'd finally fallen asleep, he had dreams about it all night.

One dream in particular was more like a nightmare as he watched a flood sweep Bonnie away from his grasp. It left him desperately wanting to talk to her. Or at least make sure she was okay.

"I need some time to figure it out." Her words replayed themselves in his head.

With a heavy sigh, Jace got dressed and cleaned up before heading downstairs. He found Noel in the kitchen, munching on a piece of cinnamon toast. "Good morning."

"Good morning to you, too." She raised an eyebrow. "You look terrible."

"Gee, thanks." He shot her an annoyed look before pouring himself a cup of coffee. "I didn't sleep much. I wish Bonnie had at least told us where she'd gone. It doesn't look like she came home again last night either."

Noel hesitated. "She's staying with her brother and his wife. She'll be back sometime this evening."

Jace was just taking another sip of coffee. He lowered the cup to stare at his sister. "You've talked to her?" Relief flooded him. "And she's okay?"

"Bonnie is my friend, and I was worried. So yeah, I texted to check on her." She picked at the crust on her toast.

"When was that?"

Noel didn't meet his eyes. "Yesterday morning."

Jace set his mug down on the table more loudly than he'd intended. Black liquid sloshed over the side to pool beneath the mug. "And you didn't think to tell me? I've been worried about her since she left!"

"Don't yell at me, Jace. I'm trying to stay out of all this. She needs space, you've made it clear you don't want to talk about it. I'm trying to do right by both of you." She sighed and dropped her toast onto a paper towel. "She ran away, and you're hiding. You two are quite the pair."

He started to argue with her but couldn't. Did Noel really think he was hiding? Maybe it was time to change that.

"I'm going to wake Gunner up so we can get dressed and go to church." He hoped Bonnie would be there. But even if she didn't go, he needed to do something. "You coming?"

Noel tried to hide her smile behind a hand but failed miserably. "Of course."

"Good."

An hour later, Jace walked into church with Gunner in his

arms and Noel by his side. They got the little boy set up in his class and walked into the worship hall. Jace immediately spotted Wyatt, Chrissy, and Gran, but Bonnie wasn't there.

He hadn't realized how much he'd hoped to see her there until the disappointment settled over him. Chrissy glanced back and saw them. She leaned in to whisper to Wyatt who turned and looked as well. He got up and strode toward them, his hand outstretched. "Jace. Glad you guys came back." He smiled at Noel. "There are some empty seats in our row, I hope you'll join us."

Noel thanked him and moved down the aisle to find a seat.

"You don't mind?" For some reason, Jace had half expected Wyatt to be angry at him on his sister's behalf. But if anything, Wyatt only appeared concerned if not a little amused.

"Not at all. Look, Bonnie's always needed space like this when she's trying to decide what to do. It can be annoying." Wyatt's eyes twinkled. "She's sorting through some things today and will be back at the ranch tonight. Just don't give her too much space after that, huh?" The worship team began to play as Wyatt clapped Jace on the shoulder. "We'd better go sit down."

Jace nodded and followed as he mulled over the other man's words. Was he telling Jace to go over and talk to Bonnie as soon as she got back? A spark of hope ignited inside him as he joined the congregation in song.

BONNIE HAD CALLED HER PARENTS ON SATURDAY MORNING TO make sure both of them were home together. Dad was off at the country club, and Mom had a meeting to play bridge with some of her friends. Bonnie ended up having to schedule an appointment with them for Sunday afternoon. Instead of letting herself sit around Wyatt's house, she'd joined him at the stables on Saturday. Then she and Chrissy baked cookies as well as cinnamon scones.

Bonnie did opt to stay home from church while her brother and sister-in-law went. Maybe she was a coward, but she couldn't quite make herself go, knowing it was possible she could run into Jace there. She was going to have to face him eventually, but she'd prefer to not do that in public.

While they were gone, she spent some time reading and praying. She wanted to be able to talk to her parents without getting angry, and that was never easy. She needed to spend some time praying for the right words and a great deal of patience.

Now she stood outside her parents' estate and stared up at its massive double front door of a house that'd never felt like home.

Nell answered the door and welcomed Bonnie in with a smile. "Hi, Bonnie. Come on in, sweetie. Your parents wanted to meet you in the sitting room."

Even though Bonnie knew every nook and cranny of the house, she followed Nell and then politely sat on the rather uncomfortable couch. "Thank you, Nell."

"You're welcome. They should be here shortly."

Bonnie clasped her hands in her lap, set them down on the couch cushion, and finally stood up again and paced over to the fireplace. An oil painting of their family hung over the mantel. She clearly remembered when the photo was taken that would later be used by the artist. No one was smiling. Mom had been stressed the whole day, while Dad had threatened all of the kids with any number of punishments if they didn't cooperate for the photo. And unlike most family photos, they were told not to smile. It was probably the easiest rule to follow that day.

Her parents entered the room then. Instead of the normal hug Bonnie might have expected, Mom motioned to the couch. "It was a surprise to hear from you, Bonnie. Why don't you make yourself comfortable?" Mom waved Nell over. "Would you please ask Leo to take my daughter's gifts and load them in the trunk of her car?" Then she motioned to Bonnie. "Give Nell your keys."

Bonnie might have argued except she did want her gifts. She handed the keys over to Nell. "Thank you."

The three of them sat in silence for several moments. With the way Mom and Dad kept staring at her, they were obviously waiting for her to speak first.

She'd rehearsed things in her head a dozen times. But now that she was here, she struggled with how to start. Especially when they watched her like that–as if they were only humoring her. *God, give me the right words to say, and please let them be receptive to them.*

"Look, I know I disappointed both of you when I decided not to continue working for you. I know it isn't what you wanted." She swallowed. "But you have to understand that, for better or worse, I inherited your stubborn personality traits even if I've chosen not to inherit your money." She smiled sincerely, hoping it would soften the blow of her words. "I'm thirty-two years old. I have a job I love, a life I'm happy living, and I don't deserve to be treated like a child anymore."

Dad's jaw clenched, and Mom leaned forward, fire in her eyes. "I don't understand how you can be this unappreciative. We gave you everything you could possibly want. Why do you turn away from us like this?"

"I wish you could see that I'm not turning away from you. I love you both. I'll always be your daughter. But you've never understood me. I'm not sure you've ever tried." She shrugged sadly. "I hate sushi. I hate big gatherings where I'm the center of attention. And I've hated them since I was a child. But that doesn't matter."

"Sometimes you have to do things you don't enjoy." Dad's voice was serious, as though he were talking about the weather.

"You're right, Dad. But on my own birthday? It's like you guys don't even know me." Bonnie couldn't understand why this was so difficult for them to grasp. She took in a slow breath. "I love being a nanny. I like making a difference in a kid's life and being the person he can count on each day. And I'm truly okay with not getting rich doing it. What is so wrong with that?"

Neither of her parents said a word. Instead, they looked at her as though she'd just announced she was an alien from another planet and had replaced their daughter years ago. She wished one of them would say something.

Since it didn't appear that they were going to, Bonnie continued. "I think I've finally realized that I can't force you to be happy with my life decisions. I can, however, ask that you respect them." She slowly drew in a breath. "I want you both to be in my life. But my inability to separate myself from your criticism may have cost me a future with Jace. That one's on me. However, I can't afford to let your negativity color my life anymore. If you can't change, it'll mean we're going to see each other a lot less often. And that'll be on you."

Both of her parents rose to their feet. Even Mom, the picture of poise, looked uncertain. Bonnie almost felt sorry for them. Because while they might be confused or conflicted, Bonnie felt better than she had in a long time when it came to her parents.

Just when she didn't think either of them were going to respond, Mom said, "I'd truly forgotten you disliked sushi.

However, I…admit…it was simply what I'd wanted to serve, and I didn't think to ask you what you would prefer." Her voice was quiet. "If it makes you feel any better, I made sure the cake was chocolate since that is your favorite."

Bonnie smiled at her. "Thank you. It truly was a delicious cake."

She wanted them to apologize. To say they'd change, or at least admit they needed to work on some things. When they said nothing else, she took her cue from them. After retrieving her bag, she lifted her hand in a sad farewell, and headed for the front door. Nell met her there with Bonnie's car keys.

"Thank you, Nell."

When she finally climbed into her car, she let out a lungful of air and sank into the seat. That could've gone a lot worse. It was probably as close to an apology as she would ever get from her mom.

She checked the time. It was late enough now that it was nearly time for dinner. She knew Wyatt and Chrissy were dying to hear how the visit went. She'd go eat dinner with them, get back to the ranch late tonight, and then convince Jace to talk to her tomorrow.

Bonnie wasn't sure what she wanted to say to him, all she knew was that she'd regret it if she didn't give them a chance.

It was after eleven before Bonnie turned onto Jace's property. Despite everything that'd happened over the last two days and not knowing how things were going to turn out with Jace, many of the worries that had been weighing on her drifted away the moment she drove onto the ranch.

The lights were on in the main house. Someone was awake. She wished she could go over and talk to Jace now, but she didn't want to risk disturbing anyone. Besides, she didn't regret leaving Clearwater this late. She, Wyatt, and Chrissy had fun eating dinner, playing a video game, and laughing. Oh, she hadn't laughed that much in a long time. It was exactly what she'd needed.

She'd try to sleep, get up for work tomorrow, and pray Jace was open to what she had to say.

She pulled her car around and parked it in front of the garage. Only then did she remember the boxes of birthday gifts in the trunk. Between them and Oreo's cage in the backseat, she'd be making several trips. "I'm going to take my bag and these leftovers in first, Oreo. I'll come back for you in a few minutes." The guinea pig only shuffled around in her cage.

Bonnie slung her bag over her shoulder, got out of the car, and reached for her keys. She put one hand on the doorknob to the garage and went to unlock it only to discover that someone had already done so. She was sure she'd locked it on Friday. Someone else had to have come in for something between then and now. She cautiously pushed the door open.

"Hello? Jace, is that you?" When no one answered, she took a tentative step inside, noting that only one light in the back was on. She reached over and flipped the switch that would turn on the overhead light as well.

In a hurry to get everything unloaded so she could kick off her shoes, Bonnie turned to go up the stairs to her apartment. It wasn't until her foot touched the first step that movement caught her eye from the other side of the garage. Her head turned, and as soon as it did, a shadow shifted.

The hair on the back of her neck stood on end at the same time as the hair on her arms. It was then that she noticed most of the large tools in the garage were missing. In addition to that, several large boxes sat open on the concrete floor, items filling them to overflowing.

Someone was stealing all of Jace's grandpa's tools!

"I thought you quit." A voice from the shadows filled the garage—a man's voice Bonnie recognized but couldn't quite place. The shadow shifted and the man stepped into the light.

"Cabe?" Disbelief stunned Bonnie. "What are you doing?" Surely there had to be an explanation. She wanted to believe maybe he'd interrupted the robbery, but the large toolbox he carried spoke otherwise.

Cabe gave her a grim look as he set the toolbox into one of the boxes. "You shouldn't have come back."

Instinct kicked in. Bonnie gripped the rails and tried to dash up the stairs to her apartment. She'd barely touched the doorknob, much less had a chance to get her keys in the lock, when footsteps bounded up the stairs.

Before she could turn, a strong arm wrapped around her waist and pulled her back. A combined scent of motor oil and manure surrounded her as Cabe dragged her back down the stairs again. "I'm afraid I can't let you call Jethro's precious grandson," the man's voice dripped with sarcasm and echoed near her ear.

Once at the bottom of the stairs, Cabe pushed her against one wall of the garage. The sneer on his face combined with the wild look in his eyes and made him nearly unrecognizable.

Bonnie stepped away from the wall, only to be shoved against it again. This time, the back of her head struck the wall behind her, causing pain in her teeth.

Cabe thought for several moments before smiling, but it didn't quite reach his eyes. "On second thought, this is perfect. I heard a rumor that you were quitting after getting into a fight with the boss." The last word was spoken with disgust. "You got upset and decided to get even with him." He grabbed her roughly by the wrists and dragged her toward a utility closet at the back of the garage.

Bonnie's head throbbed and nausea gripped her stomach as dread worked its way through her body. What was Cabe going to do? She wasn't about to wait around to see. Instead, she wrestled her hands out of his and dashed for the door and her escape from the garage. She hadn't gotten halfway there, though, before Cabe reached her and knocked her to the ground. A black ski mask landed on the floor next to her.

Cabe retrieved it and stuffed it into a back pocket. "Oh, no. Not yet, honey. First, you need to set the fire that'll burn down the garage. You know, to pay Jace back for how poorly he's treated you." His face morphed into a dramatic frown. "It's too bad you weren't smart enough to get out of the garage before you were trapped inside."

With one hand holding her wrists and the other pulling her hair, he moved her toward the closet. With a hollow laugh, he shoved her inside and slammed the door behind her.

Bonnie felt her way through the darkness back to the door as something shuffled against it outside. She turned the doorknob and pushed, but something kept it from opening.

Cabe must have blocked it with something.

Foreboding gave way to terror as she threw her body against the door. It made no difference. Tears stung her eyes as the only light in the small closet came from the gap beneath the door. "Don't do this, Cabe. Look, I'm stuck. Get out of here. You have time to be long gone before anyone else finds me." *God, help me. Please!*

Cabe said nothing.

Bonnie listened as he moved things around in the garage. At one point, all was silent, and she thought he might have left. Instead, a strange sound filtered through the door; like liquid being poured from a spout.

Suddenly, the putrid scent of gasoline began to fill the closet. Bonnie's heart jumped into her throat, and she pounded the door with her fists. "Let me go! Open the door!"

"Not on your life, honey."

Footsteps retreated. A minute of silence went by and then she saw it: The flickering light below the door that told her Cabe had set the garage on fire just like he'd promised.

Bonnie's throat went dry as she tried to swallow her fear. "Someone help me!"

Chapter Twenty

J ace spent all Sunday afternoon missing Bonnie like crazy. He'd lost count of how many times he looked out of the upstairs alcove to see if her car was parked outside the garage.

Noel caught him twice and shook her head. "You've got it bad, big brother." She nodded toward the window. "She'll be back."

"I know." The afternoon stretched into evening. Jace busied himself playing with Gunner and then getting him ready for bed. After tucking his son in for the night, he retrieved a book and went to sit in the alcove to wait for Bonnie to get home.

When her car's headlights first appeared, Jace nearly dropped the book he held. Instead, he set it down and jumped to his feet. He grabbed the baby monitor and went downstairs where Noel was watching television.

"Bonnie just pulled up." He handed the monitor to Noel. "Will you keep an ear out for Gunner? I'm going to go talk to her."

"Of course." She took it and pointed to the door. "I'll try not to stalk you both while I wait."

Jace grinned at her and playfully kicked her foot. "I appreciate that."

He went outside and jogged down the path and around the corner to where Bonnie's car was parked. Immediately, a dark figure dashed from the garage door and slid across the hood of her car as it ran.

"Stop!" Jace yelled, his deep voice carrying in the windless night. He rounded the back of her car to cut the man off.

The figure hesitated as though he were contemplating his next move. Between the poor lighting from the garage and the ski mask the man wore, it was impossible for Jace to tell who it was. He knew, though, that it had to be the same man who'd routinely caused trouble around the ranch. Jace's hand moved to touch the gun on his belt. "You aren't going anywhere."

The figure straightened a little and a broken laugh came from the mask. "You think you're in charge, don't you?"

The voice sent a stab of confusion straight to Jace's chest. "Cabe?" Surely he wasn't responsible for all of this. He was Grandpa's closest friend. "Why are you doing this?"

The man jerked his ski mask off, the anger on his face easily detectable even in the dim lighting. "Because, while you've been pampered in your office job, I worked with Jethro side-by-side for nearly thirty years. Because while you only visited once or twice a year, I worked my hands to the bone." He pointed a finger at Jace. "And how did Jethro reward me when he died? By giving this place to his rich and clueless grandson." He sneered. "I should've gotten this place." When he laughed, his voice sounded hollow. "Instead, his rich brat of a grandson gets everything handed to him on a silver platter." He pointed to the garage. "Not this time, though."

An eerie orange glow lit the windows in the garage as

smoke found ways to escape through cracks around the glass. *Bonnie!*

"It's too late. Whatever happens, you're not going to make it to her on time."

A scream came from the garage. "Help me!"

Bonnie's voice jolted Jace.

Cabe capitalized on his momentary distraction and took several steps forward. "Don't even think about it," he growled.

Jace didn't have time for this. If Bonnie was stuck in the garage, then every second counted. He withdrew his gun and leveled it at Cabe. "Back off, or I will shoot."

Cabe stared at him with wide eyes as though daring him to make good on his promise. "Go for it." When Jace didn't shoot, Cabe cackled. "That's what I thought." With that, he dove at Jace.

Jace didn't hesitate. He aimed and fired his gun, hitting Cabe in the shoulder.

The man fell to the ground, rolled over, and got up again with a hand against his arm. "Trust me, *son*, this isn't over!" He stumbled as he ran toward the tree line.

Jace let him go—he'd be easy enough to hunt down later. He heard Noel calling him from the back door.

"I'm okay! Get in the house, lock the door. Call the police and fire department. Now!"

He shoved his gun into the holster and ran for the garage. "Bonnie!" The doorknob was warm as he pulled it open and smoke billowed out. He coughed hard and tried to fan it away from his face. "Bonnie!"

"Jace! I'm here. Help me, please!"

Without hesitation, he charged into the garage. Flames licked at the cabinets that lined one side, and the heat from it was nearly unbearable.

At first, he saw no sign of her. Bonnie's frantic voice drew his attention to the closet at the back. Anger boiled to the surface, and he vowed to find Cabe once Bonnie was safe. He shoved a rolling tool chest out of the way, jerked the door open, and scooped Bonnie into his arms. "I've got you. Hold on." Her arms tightened around his neck as he sprinted for the door. All around them, flames climbed the walls and danced across the ceiling like something out of a nightmare.

When he burst into the fresh air outside, he tripped and landed on one knee. He struggled to his feet, keeping Bonnie close as she gasped and coughed against his chest, as he stumbled toward the safety of the house.

The backdoor opened and Noel leaned out, her phone to one ear. "Police and the fire department are on the way." Her eyes widened as she hurried to help Jace support Bonnie as made it to the porch. "What happened? I thought I heard a gunshot." Noel put one hand on Jace's shoulder and the other against Bonnie's back.

Jace tried to catch his breath. If the amount of smoke he'd breathed in was burning his lungs right now, how badly must Bonnie be hurting? "It was Cabe. He locked Bonnie up inside and set the garage on fire. I shot him in the shoulder." He pointed to the line of trees. "He took off that way, but I doubt he's going to get far."

Jace carried Bonnie in through the door Noel held open and set her down in a kitchen chair. He knelt in front of her and brushed the hair out of her face. Black marks smeared across her cheeks and forehead as she covered her mouth with a hand and continued to cough. "Were you burned anywhere?"

She shook her head. "No, I don't think so…" She coughed again, her voice hoarse. Tears streamed from her eyes, clearing a path through the soot on her face. "If you hadn't found me…" Her body shook, whether it was with coughing, sobs, or both, Jace couldn't tell.

He pulled her into his arms again and pressed a kiss to her hair. "You're okay."

Sirens filled the air as emergency vehicles approached the house. Jace looked to Noel. "Watch her. I have to tell them about Cabe. I'll have paramedics come in here to help Bonnie." He touched Bonnie's chin. "I'll be right back."

Outside, he was relieved to spot an ambulance among the emergency vehicles. He motioned to them. "Bonnie's in the kitchen with smoke inhalation." He noted that firemen were already preparing to fight the fire. The captain jogged over. "Is anyone else in the building?"

"No. No one."

The captain nodded as a police officer approached. Jace began to tell him about Cabe and what the man had done to Bonnie and how he'd set the fire. He coughed hard, his throat burning.

Minutes later, a police officer called out, "I found him." He clutched the collar of Cabe's black shirt in one hand while he kept his weapon pointed at him. "He has a truck full of tools and equipment on the other side of the garage."

Cabe was handcuffed and his eyes remained on the burning garage, a wide smile on his face, as the police escorted him away.

"You'll have to come with us for questioning," the first officer told Jace. Jace knew he'd have to answer a number of questions regarding his use of a firearm, but as they brought Bonnie out of the house on a wheeled stretcher, he wished with everything that he had he could be going to the hospital with her.

He jogged over to where Bonnie was lying, an oxygen mask over her face. "I'm sorry I can't ride with you, but I'll be at the hospital as soon as I can. I promise."

She nodded. Then her eyes widened, and she pulled the mask away from her mouth. "Oreo!"

Jace's stomach fell as he looked up at the garage. The entire structure was engulfed in flames. The firemen were dousing it with water, but he doubted the little guinea pig would make it through. "I'm sorry, Bonnie. I…"

"He's in the car. I didn't get a chance…to take him…back upstairs yet." She began coughing again.

Relief flooded Jace. He chuckled in spite of everything they'd just gone through. "Well, that's one lucky critter. Don't worry, we'll get him into the house." He moved the mask to cover her face again. "Hang in there, darlin'." He squeezed her hand then nodded for the medic to get her into the ambulance.

Watching the ambulance drive away while Jace was stuck at the ranch was the very definition of being pulled in two different directions.

The flames from the garage were nearly out now. Jace needed to find out how the building fared, though he suspected poor Bonnie had likely lost most of her possessions. He sure hoped he was wrong. What he needed to do right now was check on Gunner and Noel, deal with the police, and get to the hospital to check on the woman he loved.

A MOAN WAS THE FIRST THING BONNIE REGISTERED AS SHE began to wake up. Where was it coming from? The person sounded miserable. A few moments later, she realized the moan was coming from her own throat. And then it hit her.

The mother of all headaches. Her whole head throbbed. She tried to open her eyes, but the moment light hit her pupils, the headache intensified. She squeezed her eyelids shut.

Where was she? What happened?

Confusion mixed with the pain. "Jace?" She barely recognized the sound of her own voice.

Something was pinching her arm. She put a hand there and felt a tube coming out of it.

"Hey, Bonnie. I'm here." A warm hand covered her own. "You're in the hospital, and I need you to leave the IV alone."

His thumb drew circles on the back of her hand. The repetitive motion stilled her, and Bonnie tried to focus on the sound of his voice.

She was in the hospital? She struggled to remember what happened. It slowly came together. Cabe surprising her in the garage. Getting locked in the closet. The fire. And Jace coming to her rescue. If it hadn't been for him...

A hot tear escaped the corner of her eye. It didn't make it halfway down its escape route before Jace wiped it away.

"Are you hurting?"

Bonnie nodded and even that motion sent waves of pain through her head. "My. Head." She coughed, sending splinters of agony through her head and chest. Had they caught Cabe? Was the garage okay? She had so many questions, yet her throat was too scratchy and hurt too much to voice them.

"I'm going to find the nurse. I'll be right back." His hand left hers, allowing cool air to hit her skin. She wanted to tell him not to leave. A few minutes later, she heard his voice again. "Bonnie says her head hurts. She won't even open her eyes."

A woman spoke. "Bad headaches are common after smoke inhalation and exposure to carbon monoxide. We'll give her some pain medication through her IV which should help. The best thing for her is rest, continued oxygen, and time."

For the first time, Bonnie noticed the oxygen cannula in her nose as someone adjusted it.

Apparently, whatever medication the nurse had given her was working. Her head stopped pounding as hard and she began to relax as everything around her started to fade. "Jace?" Her raspy voice was barely above a whisper.

"Right here." His hand held hers again.

"So sleepy. Don't leave."

"I'm not going anywhere."

The last thing she registered was the sensation of his lips on her forehead as blissful sleep claimed her.

The next time Bonnie woke up, her head didn't hurt nearly as bad. It still took her several moments to remember where she was and what happened. But this time, when she tried to open her eyes, the light didn't make her head throb like it was going to explode.

She blinked several times and moved a little. It must have gotten Jace's attention because his face shifted into focus. When he saw her eyes were open, he smiled at her. "Hey, you. Welcome back."

Bonnie coughed, winced in response to her sore throat, and tried to clear it. "What happened...with Cabe? Did they catch him?" She coughed again.

Jace produced a small cup of water with a straw. "Here, take a sip of this. The nurse said the more you can drink the better."

Even though it hurt to swallow, the cool water felt like heaven as it coursed down her throat. "Thank you."

"You're welcome." He set the cup down again and smoothed some hair away from her forehead. "As for what happened, let's see... I was waiting for you to get home. When I saw your car arrive, I wanted to come over and talk to you even though it was late. I didn't want to wait until

Monday morning. But as I was walking to the garage, I saw Cabe running."

Bonnie listened in silence as he told her about shooting Cabe, seeing the flames, getting Bonnie out, and then the officer returning with Cabe after hunting the man down.

"Cabe will be charged for attempted murder among many other things. Between what I saw, what he told me, and what he did to you, there's no way he'll be getting out of prison any time soon."

Bonnie shook her head, the movement reminding her of the lingering headache. "I can't believe he did it all…because he hated that your grandpa willed the ranch to you and Noel instead of him." She coughed and reached for the cup of water again. After several sips, she said, "How is the garage?"

Jace's face fell. "It's not good. The fire department said we can go in after another day or two and assess the damage." Sympathy crossed his features. "I'm sorry, Bonnie. We'll go up together and see what we can salvage."

Bonnie thought about the photo albums she had, her book collection, and the special things that she'd been given at different times in her life. It might all be gone forever. Tears sprang to her eyes. At the same time, she had her life. And even Oreo was okay.

It could've been much worse.

"It'll be okay," she whispered. "Thanks for saving my life, Jace."

"Are you kidding?" He leaned in close, his nose nearly touching hers. "I'd run into a burning building for you any day of the week."

She laughed then, the motion making her cough again. She thought about the days leading up to the fire and sobered. "I'm sorry about what happened. At my parents' house." She paused as she tried to get her breath. "I was going to tell you on Monday. I don't care about money, Jace. If you have five dollars or five million." She reached up and pressed her palm to his cheek. "I don't ever want to leave you and Gunner. I'm so in love with you."

He smiled tenderly at her as he rested his hand over hers. "And I was going to tell you that I'd give it all away if that's what it took to make you stay. I love you, Bonnie. More than you'll ever know."

He kissed her gently then. A sweet, chaste kiss that made Bonnie feel warm, safe, and content.

"I'm sorry, darlin'." Jace walked up behind her and slid his arms around her waist as they surveyed the contents of her apartment. While only sections of it had actually been burned, the damage caused by water and smoke had taken its toll.

Very little was recognizable. It would be a miracle if anything could be saved.

She leaned into his chest with a sad sigh. "This is what I'd prepared myself for. But I guess I was still hoping it wouldn't be this bad."

"I know. So was I." He leaned forward and rested his chin on her shoulder. "Still, we'll comb through everything just in case. I need to do the same thing downstairs, too, although it looks like nearly everything was incinerated."

An image of Bonnie trapped in the burning garage entered his mind as it had many times since that night. He looked forward to it becoming a distant memory instead of one that triggered another round of fear and panic.

"I'm sorry about your grandpa's tools." Bonnie's voice

had gotten stronger over the last few days, but it was still a little raspy.

Jace held her tighter. "They are just things. I managed to get the most important treasure out in time." With that, he pressed a kiss to her jaw near her earlobe. He registered the remaining smoke smell in the air and steered Bonnie towards the stairs. "Come on, we need to get out of here before the fumes start to bother you again."

She didn't argue with him. The doctors said she'd make a full recovery, but it might take many weeks. Meanwhile, she was using two different inhalers and ordered to stay far away from smoke of any kind.

She'd been lucky. They both had.

Together, they made their way outside and around to the front porch. They sat on the swing, and she leaned into Jace as he put his arm around her shoulders. "You need to make a list of everything you've lost. I'm not sure how long it'll take insurance money to come in, but we'll start trying to replace what we can."

Bonnie was silent for several moments. Long enough for Jace to lean back and down to look at her face. "You okay?"

She nodded. "It's so overwhelming. You know?"

He completely understood. There'd been something he desperately wanted to ask her, but the timing hadn't been right.

Until now.

Jace shifted away from her a little and reached for her hands. He swallowed as he studied her beautiful eyes—eyes that watched him with the kind of trust and love that had his heart turning over in his chest. "Then we'll rebuild—and I'd love to do it together. I love you, Bonnie. It took me way too long to realize it, and even longer to admit it, but I can't imagine doing life without you by my side." He reached up and tucked some hair gently behind her ear. "Will you marry me?"

She nodded, a sweet smile on her face. "I want to marry you more than anything, Jace Echolls. I love you, too."

Jace gathered her in his arms and kissed her.

This. It didn't get much better than this.

Epilogue

Wyatt stepped up and held his elbow out for Bonnie. As soon as she put her arm in his, he tightened his hold. "You ready for this?"

"Absolutely." She ran a hand down the white dress that flowed over her hips and stopped just above her ankles. It fit perfectly and was elegant without being extravagant. Her hair hung around her shoulders, curled just enough to give it some bounce. Her shoes, flat Mary Janes, matched her dress yet were comfortable to wear.

When Jace asked her what kind of wedding she wanted, she'd had one word for him: Simple.

She and Wyatt approached the doors that led to the church's worship hall where the pastor, Jace, and the rest of the wedding party waited for them.

Wyatt leaned in close. "No regrets on the small wedding?"

"Not even one." The thought of trying to organize a wedding that suited her parents as well as Jace's sounded like a nightmare. This was the closest thing to eloping that they dared to do, and she was glad she'd made the decision.

They'd have a big reception in a few days where all of their family and friends could attend.

For now, she wanted to be married in the presence of the people they were closest to.

Wyatt pushed the doors open and led Bonnie through them.

She looked past the empty seats to Jace at the other end. He stood next to the pastor with little Gunner in his arms while Gran, Chrissy, and Noel waited for her on the other side.

The pastor motioned them forward.

Jace set Gunner down and Noel moved to take the boy's hand.

With each step, Bonnie's gaze stayed with Jace's. His smile expressed his wonder as she approached. Wyatt kissed her on the cheek and then moved her hand from his arm to Jace's.

"You look absolutely beautiful," Jace whispered.

Dressed in black slacks and a white button-down shirt, Jace looked amazing himself. She blushed as they turned to face the pastor.

Bonnie soaked the moment in as he began the ceremony. As they said their vows, she knew that no matter what came their way, they'd be able to face it together.

When it was time for the rings, Jace turned to Gunner, who handed him a box with Noel's help. "Thanks, buddy," he said as he withdrew the rings.

Once both were nestled on their fingers, they turned to face each other as the pastor said, "I now declare you husband and wife. You may kiss the bride."

Jace wasted no time in taking her into his arms and kissing her until their friends and family started to giggle and clap.

When their kiss broke, Bonnie smiled up at her new

husband. "I hope it's always like this, and that we never argue again."

Jace chuckled. "I hope so, too. If we do, I'll bet making up is going to be a whole lot more fun." He winked and kissed her again as her cheeks warmed.

Bonnie sighed with contentment. She'd rather argue and make up with Jace than get along with anyone else.

§&

THANK YOU SO MUCH FOR READING **MARRYING BONNIE**. I hope you'll consider leaving a review. Stay tuned, because Emma and Noel will both be getting books of their own!

If you enjoyed these books, I think you'll love the Love's Compass series! Check out the first, Finding Peace, today!

TUCK IS DETERMINED TO KEEP LAURIE SAFE, EVEN IF IT **means risking his own heart in the process.**

Police Officer Tuck Chandler works hard to protect the citizens of Kitner, Texas. He's also good at holding women at arm's length. Jilted by his fiancée for his dedication to his job, he's not about to open himself up to hurt like that again.

Laurie Blake is a struggling photographer. After growing up in a wealthy family, she's determined to make it on her own, even if it means doing it the hard way.

When Tuck is assigned to a puzzling burglary involving Laurie's fledgling photography business, he goes into it with his usual perseverance. He wants to help her – if she'll let him. As the case unfolds and the mystery deepens, another question arises.

Will their pasts get in the way of a future together?

Read it now!

Want a FREE BOOK?

Sign up for Melanie D. Snitker's newsletter and get her novella, *Finding Forever in Romance*, **FREE!**

Sign up today!

Special Thanks

I want to thank you, my wonderful readers, for your patience over the last year or two as releases haven't been as frequent. Many of you know that our son has severe autism as well as epilepsy, and that we've faced a lot of challenges. Thankfully, while things aren't easy, I now have time to write most days. I look forward to releasing books more regularly again.

Many thanks to Kris, Rachel, and Steph for their incredibly valuable suggestions. Ladies, I can't say enough how much I appreciate you.

Krista, you are more than an editor, you are a miracle worker! Thanks for your time, comments, and advice.

There are a number of amazing people on my ARC team that took the time to read this book. Thank you all! I'd especially like to mention Kati, Amber, Teresa, Sarah, and Alice.

And last but not least, thank you, Doug, for your unending support. I'm so blessed that we can do life together. I love you!

About the Author

Melanie D. Snitker has enjoyed writing fiction for as long as she can remember. She started out writing episodes of cartoon shows that she wanted to see as a child and her love of writing grew from there. She and her husband live in Texas with their two children, who keep their lives full of adventure. They also have two dogs and a guinea pig who add a dash of mischief to the family dynamics. In her spare time, Melanie enjoys photography, reading, crochet, baking, and hanging out with family and friends.

https://www.melaniedsnitker.com/
https://www.facebook.com/melaniedsnitker
https://twitter.com/MelanieDSnitker
https://www.instagram.com/melaniedsnitker/

Books by Melanie D. Snitker

Healing Hearts

Calming the Storm

I Still Do

Life Unexpected Complete Series

Safe In His Arms

Someone to Trust

Starting Anew

Love's Compass Complete Series

Finding Peace

Finding Hope

Finding Courage

Finding Faith

Finding Joy

Finding Grace

Books by Melanie D. Snitker

Brides of Clearwater

Marrying Mandy

Marrying Raven

Marrying Chrissy

Marrying Bonnie

Sage Valley Ranch

Charmed by the Daring Cowboy

Welcome to Romance

Fall Into Romance

A Merry Miracle in Romance

www.ingramcontent.com/pod-product-compliance
Lightning Source LLC
Chambersburg PA
CBHW020410210626
46816CB00006BB/2213